MISTAKES WERE MADE

A *New York Times* Bestseller

"Seldom has failure been so likeable—or so funny."
—***The Wall Street Journal***

"Pastis has assembled an eccentric and funny cast . . . yet there are also touching interactions to be found." —***Publishers Weekly***

"Fans of the Wimpy Kid series will enjoy this book." —***Parade***

"Readers should be simultaneously amused and touched by this quirky antihero." —***Booklist***

"Top-notch stuff." —***A Fuse #8 Production***

"An unforgettable protagonist whose unorthodox approach to detective work (and world domination) will have readers in stitches."
—**Lincoln Peirce, creator of the Big Nate series**

"Immortalized in ink on the sole of my left shoe are the words I HEART TIMMY."
—**Tess Riesmeyer, Penguin Bookshop, Sewickley, PA**

MISTAKES WERE MADE

STEPHAN PASTIS

CANDLEWICK PRESS

This is a work of fiction. Names, characters, places,
and incidents are either products of the author's
imagination or, if real, are used fictitiously.

First movie tie-in edition 2020

Library of Congress Catalog Card Number 2012942409
ISBN 978-0-7636-6050-5 (hardcover)
ISBN 978-0-7636-6927-0 (paperback)
ISBN 978-1-5362-0907-5 (movie tie-in paperback)

20 21 22 23 24 25 MNG 10 9 8 7 6 5 4 3 2 1

Printed in Saline, MI, U.S.A.

This book was typeset in Nimrod.
The illustrations were done in pen and ink.

Candlewick Entertainment
an imprint of
Candlewick Press
99 Dover Street
Somerville, Massachusetts 02144

www.candlewick.com

To my uncle George Mavredakis.
Thank you for everything.

A Prologue That Story-wise Is Out of Order

It's harder to drive a polar bear into some-body's living room than you'd think. You need a living-room window that's big enough to fit a car. You need a car that's big enough to fit a polar bear. And you need a polar bear that's big enough to not point out your errors. Like the fact that you've driven into the wrong house. Which, when it comes to cars in living rooms, is bad.

I should back up.

(The story. Not the car.)

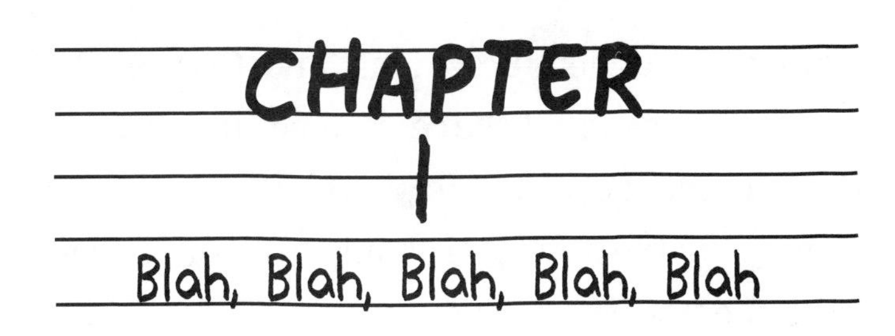

All right, let's get the boring stuff out of the way. My name is Failure. Timmy Failure. I look like this:

My family name was once Fayleure. But somebody changed it. Now it is spelled as you see. I'd ask that you get your "failure" jokes out of the way now. I am anything but.

I am the founder, president, and CEO of the detective agency I have named for myself: Failure, Inc. Failure, Inc., is the best detective agency in the town, probably the state. Perhaps the nation.

The book you are holding is a historical record of my life as a detective. It has been rigorously fact-checked. All the drawings in here are by me. I tried to get my business partner to do the illustrations, but they were not good. For example, here is his depiction of me:

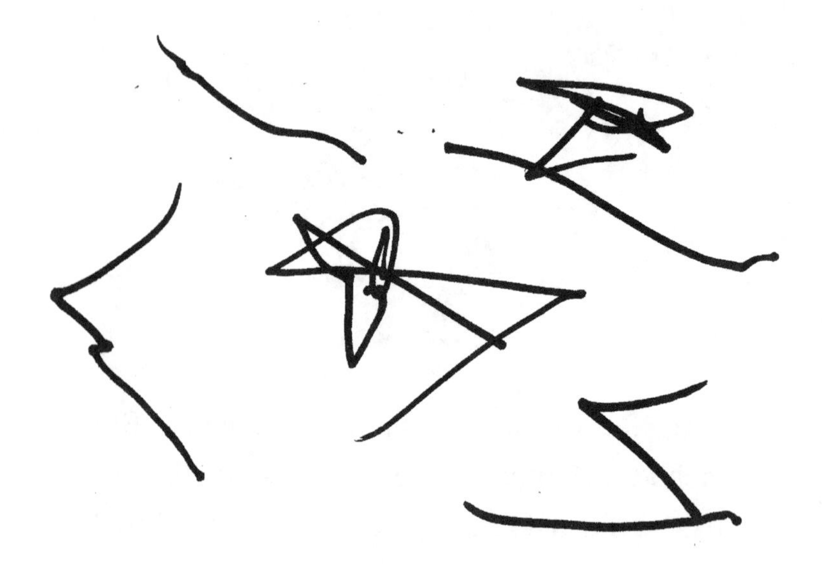

I have decided to publish this history because my expertise is invaluable to anyone who ever wanted to be a detective. Just read the reviews:

> **"Invaluable to anyone who ever wanted to be a detective."**
>
> **—Anonymous**

But success did not come overnight for me. I had to overcome obstacles. Like these:

1. my mother
2. my school
3. my idiot best friend
4. my polar bear

And yes, I'm sure you have the same question everyone else does when I list these obstacles. Why am I best friends with an idiot? I'll get to it later. Oh, and I suppose I should say a word about the fifteen-hundred-pound polar bear.

His name is Total.

Total's Arctic home is melting. So he wandered for food and found my cat dish. He is now 3,101 miles from his former home. Yes, that's a long way to roam for a cat dish, but we buy good cat food. Sadly my cat is now in Kitty Heaven (or perhaps the Kitty Badlands—he never was a friendly cat), but I still have the polar bear.

Initially Total displayed a fair degree of diligence and reliability, and thus I agreed to make him a partner in my agency. As it turned out, the diligence and reliability were a ruse. Something polar bears do. And I don't want to talk about it. I also don't want to discuss the change I agreed to make to the name of the agency, which now reads like this in our yellow pages ad:

> **TOTAL FAILURE, INC.**
>
> **(WE WON'T FAIL, DESPITE WHAT THE NAME SAYS.)**

And now I have to go. Because the Timmyline is ringing.

CHAPTER 2

The Candy Man Can't 'Cause He's Missing All His Chocolate

The call is from Gunnar. Classmate, neighbor, and now just another guy missing his Halloween candy. I get a lot of candy cases. They're not headline grabbing, but they pay cash money. So I wake up my partner and hop on the Failuremobile.

I should say a word about the Failuremobile. It's not actually called a Failuremobile.

It's called a Segway. And it belongs to my mother. She won it in a raffle. And she has set forth some restrictions on when and how I can use it.

I thought that was vague. So I use it. So far, she hasn't objected. Mostly because she doesn't know.

That touches upon one of the founding principles of Total Failure, Inc., which I've memorialized in ink on the sole of my left shoe.

The only complaint I have about the Failuremobile is its speed. If I ride it somewhere while Total walks, Total gets there first. That wouldn't be so bad if it weren't for the fact that in between, Total naps.

So it isn't any surprise to me that when I get to Gunnar's house, Total is already there, doing something that he frequently does when he beats me to a house. Before I tell you what that is, let me just say this: first impressions are critical in the detective world. A client has to know at first glance that their detective is (a) professional, (b) classy, and (c) discreet.

All of this is undermined when the client's first impression of their detective is this:

I've lectured Total so many times on eating garbage from clients' trash cans that I now believe he is purposely sabotaging the agency. Fortunately for me, by the time I knock on Gunnar's door, Total has finished eating everything edible from the trash cans and is able to stand next to me on the porch.

Gunnar answers the door and escorts us to the scene of the crime. He points to an empty table by his bed. "My plastic pumpkin filled with candy was right there," he says while pointing at the tabletop. "Now it's gone."

I look at the tabletop. I can tell from the empty space that it is gone.

He starts listing the candy he had in the pumpkin. “Two Mars bars, a Twix, seven 3 Musketeers, five Kit Kats, eleven Almond Joys, five Snickers, an Abba-Zaba, and eight Hershey’s Kisses.”

Gunnar looks up at me. “You getting all this down?”

“ ’Course I’m getting it down.”

"Let's start with the basics," I tell the client, "like payment. I take cash, checks, and credit cards." I don't actually take credit cards, but it sounds professional, so I say it.

"How much will it cost?" asks the client.

"Four dollars a day, plus expenses."

"Expenses?" asks Gunnar.

"Chicken nuggets for the big man," I say, pointing up at Total. Total roars, which looks intimidating until he falls backward and crushes Gunnar's desk.

That, I know, will be coming out of his chicken nuggets. I tell Gunnar that I anticipate a six-week investigation. Lot of witnesses. Maybe some air travel.

"I'll show myself out," I tell him.

As I walk down the hall, I pass his brother Gabe's room. Gabe is sitting on his bed, surrounded by candy wrappers. There is chocolate smeared all over his face and an empty plastic pumpkin on the floor.

Always on the lookout for clues, I make an important note in my detective log.

CHAPTER 3

The Timmy Empire Strikes Back

All I need to solve the Gunnar case is five minutes of peace. But I can't get it. Because of this man.

He is Old Man Crocus. He is my teacher.

And he stands at his beloved whiteboard for six hours a day to tell me things that could bore the fur off a squirrel.

Old Man Crocus is 187 years old. He smells. And he is bent over like he's got a sack of potatoes hanging from his forehead.

That would be useful if I were making French fries. But I'm not. I'm building a detective agency empire. And there is nothing in my classroom that is going to help me get there. Except maybe the world map on the wall. Which is why I've taken it and filled in all the territories that will have Total Failure offices within five years.

A good teacher would reward that sort of initiative. But not Old Man Crocus. He says,

"What has Captain Thickhead done now?" and eliminates my hard work with correction fluid.

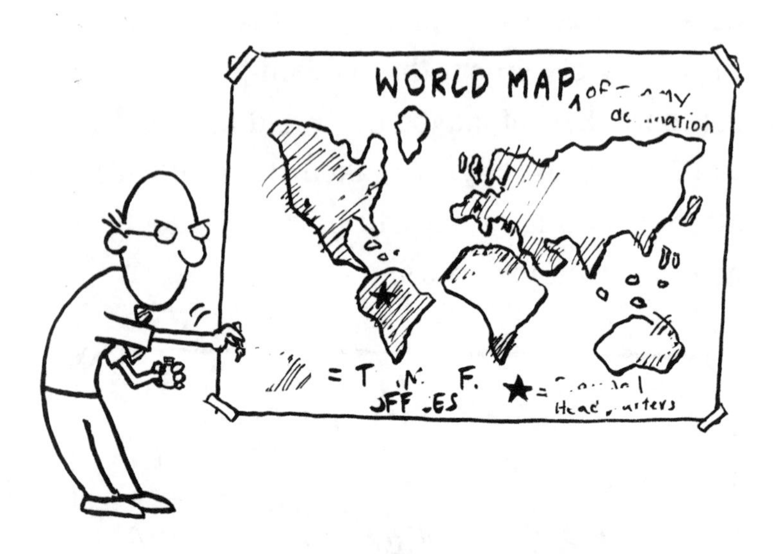

So I take my face and eliminate his.

I think that's tit for tat, but he sees it differently. So he moves me to a grouping of desks with the three "smart" kids in the hope that they'll rub off on me. They're surely hoping that *I* rub off on *them*.

One of them is Molly Moskins. She is a nuisance. She smiles too much. And she smells like a tangerine.

The rotund boy is Rollo Tookus. We have plenty of time, so we can talk about him later.

And the girl whose face I've obscured is someone I am never ever, ever, ever going to talk about ever, no matter what.

So fine, let's talk about the rotund boy.

CHAPTER 4

Meet Rollo Tookus

The first thing you need to know about Charles "Rollo" Tookus is that he is not smart. Yes, he has a 4.6 grade-point average, but that is only because he studies. Obsessively.

If *I* studied, my GPA would also be 4.6, instead of what it currently is, which is .6 (if I round up). Why Rollo studies as Rollo studies is a mystery to everyone but Rollo.

If you ask him about it, he'll yammer on about how if he studies, he'll get good grades, and how if he gets good grades, he can one day get into a university called Stanfurd, and how if he gets into Stanfurd, he can get a good job and make lots of money. Detectives have a word for that.

BORING

In fact, that brings up another one of the founding principles of Failure, Inc., one which I've memorialized on the sole of my *right* shoe.

I'd feel sorry for the poor kid if he had a parent *making* him do all this, but he doesn't.

He *chooses* to do it. Which proves he's not smart. So the best I can do is to be supportive. Try not to criticize his deficiencies. Which can be hard when I hang out in his room and kick my feet up.

Unwinding in Rollo's room at the end of a long day at the agency is one of the ways I support him. I tell him about the cases I'm working on, and he studies. I think it's exciting for him to hear my stories. After all, it's obvious that Rollo would be a detective if he could. He just doesn't have the tools. That of course doesn't stop him from making amateurish comments about my cases, which can get very annoying.

Like today. I mentioned the Gunnar case and how he has a messy brother named Gabe, and Rollo said perhaps the stupidest thing he's ever said about one of my cases. Which was this:

"Maybe Gabe ate the candy."

Told you he was an idiot.

CHAPTER 5

Problems at the Office

Day Two on the Gunnar case. No leads. Office tense. Total and I know that the best thing to do in these situations is to give each other some space. Which is hard given that our office is my mother's closet.

Corporate Headquarters

The office wouldn't be nearly as cramped if my mother would get rid of all her clothes. I scheduled a teleconference with her over dinner last week to discuss it. Here's how it went:

That's how it is in business sometimes. You try to compromise, but other parties make it difficult.

I think it's because she's stressed. I'm not sure about what. I just know it must be something, because after our teleconference that night, she took her Segway for a ride around the block. That's her way of relaxing.

“This thing is a lifesaver,” she said one time as she scooted past me. “I don’t know what I’d do without it.”

And that, my friends, is why I don’t tell her it doubles as the Failuremobile.

But right now I have a business to conduct. And my cramped office conditions must be alleviated. So I’ve asked Total to look into a possible lawsuit against my mother. I’ve even given him some law books. So far all he’s done is this:

While the space issue is a nuisance, it is actually only temporary. That's because I have my eye on the top floor of a new high-rise downtown. It has a view of the whole city.

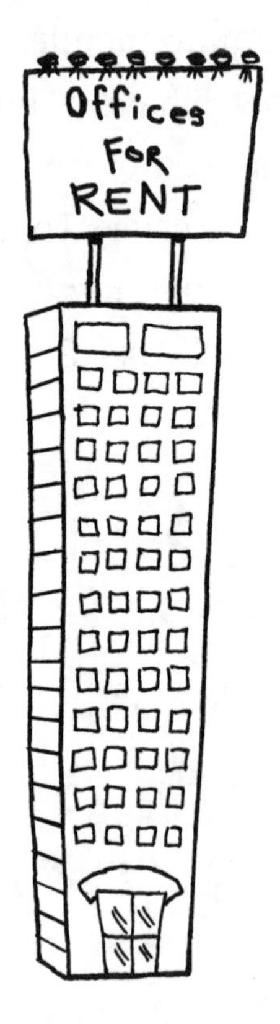

According to an ad in the newspaper, the rent is $54,000 a month. That's steep, but if the Gunnar case goes well, it'll be a drop in the bucket.

That's the way the detective business is. You crack a big case. Word spreads. Bingo bango, you're making billions. But until then, the agency will have to get its work done amid my mother's clothes. And to be fair, the rent *is* reasonable (currently $0.00), and the only restriction upon us is my mother's rule that we cannot touch her clothes.

Which shouldn't be a problem.

For me, anyway.

CHAPTER 6

It Ain't Me, Gabe

With the Gunnar investigation stalled, I do something to humor Rollo Tookus. I take a statement from Gabe, aka the Slob. "Where were you on the night your brother's candy disappeared?"

"I was in my bedroom."

"Doing what?" I ask.

"Eating," he says.

"What were you eating?" I ask.

"Candy," he says.

That's when it hits me. The import of what he is saying.

So I make a note of it in my detective log.

Can't be
Gabe.
He has
alibi.

CHAPTER 7

Sad-Eyed Lady of the Lunch Recess

Lunch recess is the only opportunity I have to do global strategy planning for the agency. So I eat on a bench by myself. It is the only way I can ensure that the other kids don't see my work and commit an act of industrial espionage.

It is pitiful, though. Pitiful that as I sit there and concentrate, my business partner groans and moans behind a chain-link fence.

The school won't let him in. So he has to stand there until I finish the school day and walk him home. He doesn't talk about it much, but I know he finds it discriminatory. To protest the school's actions, I sometimes put a sign on him.

When lunch is over, we have fifteen minutes to play whatever we want. Most kids play kickball. I sit by the fence and pet Total.

And don't ask me about the girl whose face I've obscured in the illustration. She's the same girl as before, and I still don't want to talk about her. What I will talk about is the fact that my sitting by the fence is hard on the other schoolchildren.

Hard because I am popular and they want to spend time with me. But they can't because they are wary of my Arctic business partner. Which is prudent. Polar bears are fierce and unpredictable. Plus they are always on the lookout for seals, which a schoolchild bundled up for winter can resemble.

Which is which?

The only person who is not afraid of Total is the yard lady, Dondi Sweetwater. She's a nice enough woman. But she talks quite a bit. Plus she has absolutely no concept of the time pressures I am under due to the agency.

Total, on the other hand, can't say enough good things about her. That's because she's always giving me Rice Krispies Treats to pass on to him.

Total goes bonkers for those things. And that's a real problem. Because one day we could be captured and interrogated for trade secrets and someone could offer him a Rice Krispies Treat and who knows what that fat bear would do.

For that reason, I have asked Dondi to never share this vulnerability with anyone outside the agency. I've also asked her to never even say the words *Rice Krispies Treats* aloud but to refer to said items as "the goods." She has agreed to all my stipulations and, at my request, has put her assent in writing.

TOTAL'S FONDNESS FOR "THE GOODS" IS CLASSIFIED AND SHALL REMAIN SO.

SO SWEARS
Dondi
The Yard Lady

I had to make her put it in writing because that poor woman really does like to talk. Especially to me. Which is why we spend most recesses together. But that's okay.

It's all part of being popular.

CHAPTER 8

Once Upon an Iceberg

At home that night, my detective's intuition tells me something is wrong. I've seen my mother pass in front of the house eight times on her Segway.

The previous record was six. So I know it is serious.

That night, I tell her she doesn't have to read to me in bed like she normally does. But she wants to do it anyway. She's a trouper that way.

Now, if I had my preference, I'd have her read me trade journals every night so I could keep up on the latest developments in detective technology. But someone big and furry says it's boring.

My business partner prefers a very particular type of story, one that is hard to find in most commercial bookstores. So to humor him, I am forced to handwrite the stories myself and give them to my mother to read. I even have to illustrate them. Here's how they all start:

And they all have to end the same way too, or he gets very upset and can't sleep soundly.

When she's done reading, my mom turns out the light and kisses me on the nose. I pull the blanket up to my chin and sneak a look at my business partner.

He liked the story.

CHAPTER 9

Sumo Interlude

I am up bright and early the next morning. And I am hiding behind a tree wearing a sumo suit.

I am waiting for a four-foot-tall female whose name shall not be uttered. When she passes, I am going to crash into her. With any luck, I will roll her into the curb.

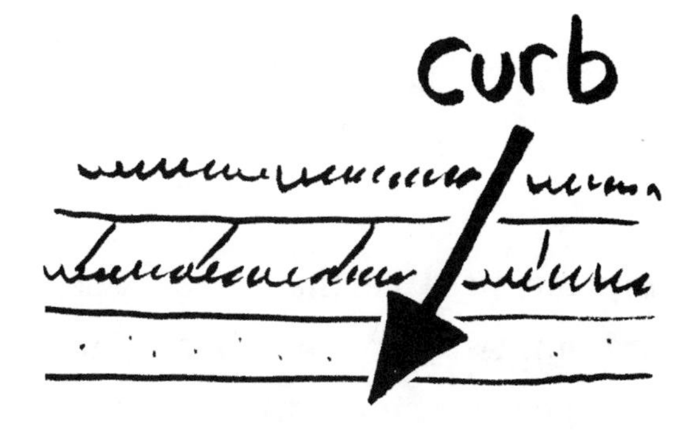

It's not personal.

It's business. And I don't want to go into it.

CHAPTER 10

More Office Problems

I ask my business partner to do one thing while I'm out. Answer the phones. And there he is, wrapped in phone cord, with the end of the line ripped out of the wall.

It's days like this that make me question his commitment. As if that's not enough, there's a note from my mom on the office door. I know she senses the agency's rising fortunes, so I assume it's a job application. But it's not.

That's the thing about my mother. She'd rather I waste an entire day at school than spend the afternoon doing sumo surveillance. I don't think she means to be misguided. I think it's the stress. She works full-time at a stationery store. And it doesn't pay super-well, so she worries a lot. I suspect that has something to do with what's been wrong with her lately.

Fortunately for her, she gave birth to a genius. A genius who will one day save the entire Failure clan (me, her, and even the polar bear, though he does not deserve salvation).

But for me to do my thing and create a multibillion-dollar detective agency, I need her to do one thing: fend off all time-wasting distractions.

By that I mean school. And on that count, she is failing.

I've asked her for a teleconference to discuss this and other things, but she is constantly rescheduling. I'm not pushing the issue for now, but I expect it will come up at her year-end review. That's the annual meeting where I sum up her strengths and weaknesses as a mother.

The way she is pushing this whole school thing is definitely going to hurt her review. But it won't be the worst review I give out this year.

That will be to this guy:

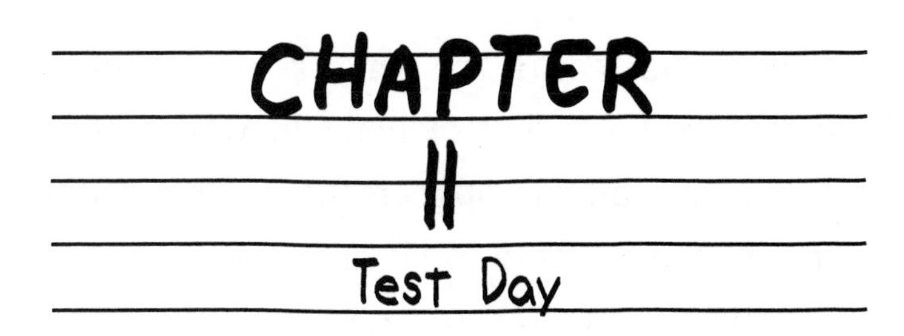

It is test day. Multiple choice. So each of us has been given a stupid Scantron form where we fill in the bubbles to indicate our answers, A through E. I am going to use the bubbles to make a picture. Last time it was mountains.

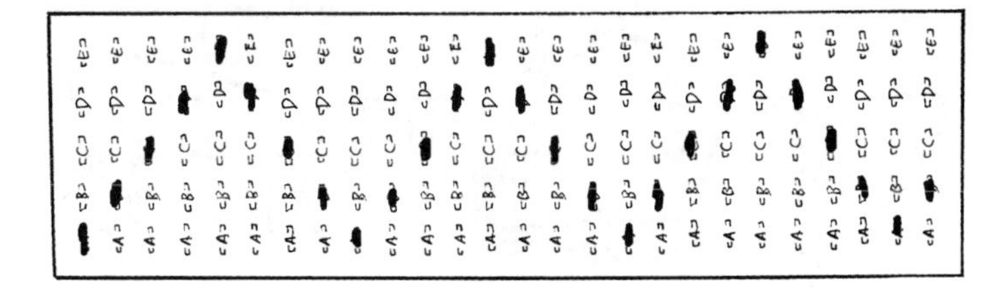

With the rest of the time, I will work on agency business. That's when Old Man Crocus says he has an announcement. "For today's test, you are going to work in groups."

Rollo Tookus's eyes widen.

"Each group will turn in one test and get one grade."

Rollo gasps.

"The group you are seated with will be your group."

Rollo takes one look at me. And passes out.

I take no notice of Rollo. For I am focused on having to join forces with the One Whose Name Shall Not Be Uttered. So I express my opinion respectfully.

Rollo moans from the floor. Old Man Crocus shouts for me to get off the desk. Molly Moskins claps. It is something she does each time she gets to work with me.

Molly's clapping sends waves of tangerine smell everywhere. Soon we all smell like tangerine people.

Old Man Crocus shuts his eyes in frustration. He grits his worn wooden teeth.

He is one unhappy tangerine.

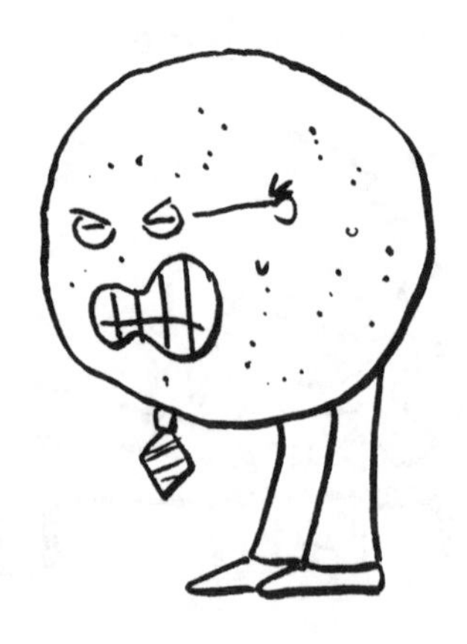

CHAPTER 12

Why Fuzzy-Wuzzy Wasn't

The one thing about the detective business is that it doesn't stop for you to solve the cases you've already got, like that of Gunnar's mysterious candy.

You just have to keep going. You can't crawl into some corner and give up.

Which is exactly what Max Hodges's hamster appears to have done.

"I found him like this when I got up this morning," Max tells me as I stand in his bedroom. "So I called you to see if you can figure out how he died."

Together we stare at the motionless hamster in the hamster cage.

"How do you know he's not alive?" I ask.

"Well," he says, handing me a photo, "because when he's alive, he looks like this."

Which is different than how he looks now.

So I ask Max the obvious. The stuff even an amateur detective knows to ask in a dead hamster case. "Did he have any enemies?"

Max says no.

"Did he have a lot of money?"

No.

"Was he depressed?"

No.

"Was he involved in criminal activity?"

No.

When it comes to crime, witnesses can clam up. So if you're a detective in these situations, you gotta put some of your own pressure on the witness. "Not involved in criminal activity," I say sarcastically. "Then what is this?" I point at a bit of hamster tube that appears to have a name scratched into it.

"I scratched my name on there," says Max.

"Looks like hamster graffiti to me," I say.

"It's not," he says.

So I grab the piece of hamster tube and put it in my pocket.

"Evidence," I say.

I show myself to the door, but when I go to open it, it won't budge. I duck low, expecting an ambush. That's when I see Total lying on the other side of it. His fat body is blocking the door.

I rap on the window with my fist until he moves, then walk to the curb to get on the Failuremobile.

The one my mother cherishes.

The one she said I can't use.

The one that isn't there.

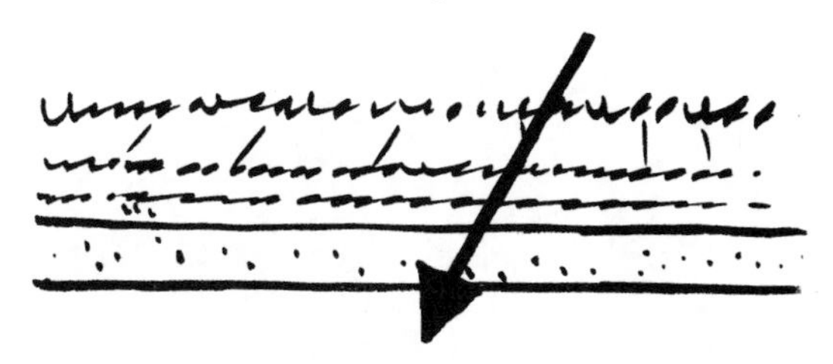

I pause to jot a brief note in my detective log.

CHAPTER 13

The Small Business Community Is Under Siege

It's hard to focus on industrial sabotage when you're sitting at a parent-teacher conference. But this much I know. Somebody somewhere needed Total Failure, Inc., stopped. Our growing caseload was simply too much of a threat. So to stop us, they seized my mode of transportation.

The obvious move is to set up a security perimeter around the neighborhood and begin questioning witnesses. But I cannot. Because I am bookended by two amateurs who have never run a business.

To my left is my mother, who made me get in the car as soon as I got back from Max Hodges's house. To my right is Old Man Crocus. All I can think as he yaps is that the man has been teaching too long.

I say that because for the first time in his 150-year career, he faces the very real possibility that he will not advance all of his students to the next grade.

I suppose here would be a good place to tell you about the student who threatens that streak.

It's moments like this when I patiently wait for my mother to impress me with a spirited defense of her son. Maybe throw around some papers. Kick over a chair. Set fire to a desk.

Instead, she nods.

For a woman who is one day going to be begging me for a job, she's doing a miserable job of impressing me.

So for now, I have to depend on my business partner, who I asked to do some reconnaissance in my absence. That means scoping out the scene of the crime and gathering information in a discreet way that does not draw attention.

It does not mean that which I found him doing when I returned home:

CHAPTER 14

Orange Juice. Shaken. Not Stirred.

I am pacing Rollo Tookus's room like a man possessed. Because when you're a detective, you cannot be the victim of an unsolved crime. It is like a dentist with missing teeth. Or a gardener with dead flowers. And dead is what I will be if my mother finds out the Failure-mobile is gone.

So I hatch a plan to keep my mother from knowing. On paper, it looks like this:

But I can't focus. Because Rollo's head is rattling back and forth like a dashboard bobblehead. It is something that happens the night before every test.

He is especially nervous tonight because he did not do well on his last test. The group test. And that was because someone in the group made the Scantron form look like this.

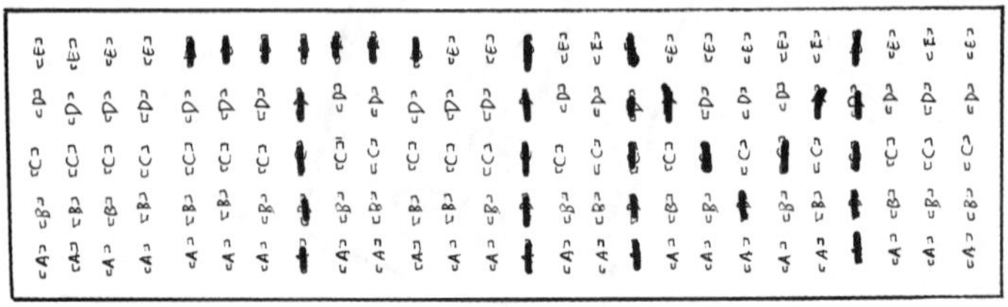

I had to do it.

If Old Man Crocus was going to pair me with You-Know-Who, I had no choice but to throw myself upon the gears of the machinery and make the whole wretched process come to a halt.

Naturally Rollo didn't see it that way. His vision is too narrow. But not me. I see the big picture. And I know that sometimes you just have to take one for the team.

One day he'll thank me for that. But not tonight. Tonight the poor kid's head is shaking like the tail of an espresso-sipping rattlesnake.

Which reminds me.

One day I will think far enough ahead to tie one of the cartons of orange juice I drink from every morning to Rollo's head. It says, SHAKE WELL BEFORE POURING.

That would look like this:

And that is why I don't worry when I have a bad string of luck as a detective.

I know I could always be an inventor.

CHAPTER 15

Please Don't Squeeze the Detective

"Man's inhumanity to man is a difficult thing to behold."

—Timmy Failure

I still must get to work. So I have a new ride. I call it the Totalmobile.

My business partner believes it is demeaning. I believe he's lucky to be employed.

I wrote *Greatness* on the side so that when people see us, they will know that we are great.

But that greatness did not prepare me for what I would see at the Weber residence.

For today it is the scene of total devastation. All marred by the remnants of someone inhumane. Someone determined. Someone whose weapon of choice comes in packs of six, twelve, and twenty. If you are squeamish, look away.

Toilet paper. It is everywhere.

And much of it hangs from the tops of trees, which tells me that these criminals were adept tree climbers. That's a major clue, and I make a note of it in my log.

I knock on the Webers' door. Jimmy Weber answers. He is in my grade.

"How's the family holding up?" I ask.

"Fine," Jimmy says. "It's not the first TP job we've ever seen."

"TP," I repeat to myself. I make another note in my log.

I ask Jimmy for a complete list of his enemies.

"Enemies?" he says. "I don't have any."

"Everyone has 'em," I tell him.

"No, really, I'm friends with everyone. People in my class. People on my soccer team. People that work with me on the school paper."

Bingo.

"I want a complete list of all the stories you've written," I tell him.

"Stories?" he asks.

"For the paper," I say.

"Oh, I don't really write stories. I just write what they're serving in the cafeteria this week. Why does that matter?"

I shake my head in disbelief. I try to remind myself that not everyone's a detective. "Listen, kid," I say. "Someone doesn't want that information out there."

"Who?" he asks.

I point to the hanging toilet paper.

"Someone who doesn't play games."

I go to hand him my card.

"Hey, Timmy, thanks, but I don't need your help anymore."

"What are you talking about?" I say. "You called the hotline."

"Yeah, over an hour ago. You took a while to show up."

It's true. I was late. Total fell asleep in front of my bedroom door, and I couldn't get out, which was very unprofessional on Total's part.

"Yeah, well I'm here now and I'm on the case," I tell him.

"Sorry," he says, "but I hired another detective. I hired—"

Don't say the name. Don't say the name. Don't say the name. Don't say the name. Don't say the name. Don't say the name. Don't say the name. Don't say the name.

"Corrina Corrina."

He says the name.

CHAPTER 16

The Chapter I Was Hoping to Put Off. The One About the Beast.

Some evil looks like Genghis Khan.

Some evil looks like Attila the Hun.

And some evil looks like this:

I really don't want to spend any more time writing about the Center of Evil in the Universe than I have to. First, because I spend absolutely no time thinking about her. And second, because I really, really hate her.

So let's be brief: The Beast owns a detective agency, the CCIA, which according to her, stands for "Corrina Corrina Intelligence Agency." I say it stands for "Corrina Corrina Is Asinine."

It is the worst detective agency in the town, probably the state. Perhaps the nation. Sadly, people are lured into hiring her by the look of her downtown office, which her rich, real-estate mogul father lets her use. It used to be a bank. It has pillars and a marble floor and a large safe. It looks like this:

As you can see, it's pathetic. And for those of us in the business, it screams, "Amateur." The stupidest, most unprofessional thing about it is that it is on the ground floor. That means that when I move into the top floor of my downtown high-rise, I will be able to throw things at her.

Making the situation even more ridiculous, the sad little girl has a huge stockpile of high-tech surveillance equipment, all furnished by her father. Cameras with zoom lenses, high-power binoculars, hidden microphones—you name it.

Now, maybe that seems impressive to you, but believe me, to someone skilled in the business, it says one thing:

SHe needs it.

Because real detectives do surveillance the old-fashioned way. With their own two eyes. And from all sorts of undesirable locales, such as laundry hampers. Which is a problem when your mother needs to do the laundry a day earlier than you expected.

CHAPTER 17

A Change Is Gonna Come

If you take one thing away from this chapter, let it be this: Timmy Failure does not lose a client to Corrina Corrina.

What she's done in taking the Weber file from me was unethical, illegal, and immoral. As a result, I have filed a complaint with the Better Detective Bureau. It is not the first such complaint I have filed against her. It is the 147th.

Because I do not own a computer or a typewriter, I have to handwrite the complaints on notebook paper. Here is one I filed last month:

Here is one I filed the week after:

I do not even know where Turkmenistan is. But it sounds far away.

Sometimes my complaints are more brief and to the point.

And sometimes my complaints are of the follow-up variety.

While these complaints are pending, I am also making two big changes to the agency. First, I bought a hat.

Please do not ask why it says BISCUITS. I do not know. Perhaps the prior owner sold biscuits. The point is that it makes me look more professional.

The second change is more substantive. I'm giving out free cheese.

So far, business is booming. At least for the free cheese.

Although everyone keeps asking me the same stupid question.

I am sitting in my room. My mother made me.

I have two spelling tests tomorrow. And she wants me to study.

But I can't. Because of the Failuremobile.

Yesterday my mother said she was going to the garage to get it so she could take it for a spin around the block. I told her not to because there are spiders in the garage.

She told me she wasn't afraid of spiders.

I told her that I didn't mean to say *spiders*. I meant to say *giant anaconda*.

She dropped the topic and hasn't brought it up again. But I can't keep coming up with Amazonian reptiles. Eventually she is going to catch on. And before she does, I've got to get the Failuremobile. All of which means redoubling my prior efforts and putting significant resources into the search. Resources which Total Failure, Inc., may or may not have. So I grab the agency's accounting records for the last six months.

The records are one of the tasks I gave to Total when he came on board. I trusted him because (a) I did not have the time to do them myself and (b) he indicated to me that he had some accounting experience.

I thus expected that the books would accurately reflect Total Failure, Inc.'s gross revenue and expenditures for the fiscal year, all neatly added and subtracted in rows and columns. Like this:

But that is not what they look like. They look like this:

I search for my accountant.

I find him sitting on the heating vent.

Eating the free cheese.

I schedule a teleconference with my mother.

CHAPTER 19

The Answer, My Friend, Is Blowing on My Ear

"I need an administrative assistant," I tell my mother.

She is at the kitchen table. It is covered in bills.

"If you want me to study for school *and* run the agency, there's no other way."

She doesn't say anything, so I ask again.

"Listen. If you just float me the funds at a reasonable rate of interest, I can hire said administrative assistant."

She turns her head toward me. "Timmy, the stationery store cut back my hours. So right now I'm a little short of said funds."

I stare at the mess of paper on the kitchen table and pick up one of the credit card bills. In big bold letters, it says this:

TOTAL AMOUNT PAST DUE: $1485.23

"This is it?" I say, holding out the bill.

"This is what?" she asks.

"These sums," I say. "They're trifling."

I hold up the phone bill, the gas bill, and a doctor bill.

"With the amount of money Total Failure, Inc., will be taking in by the end of the fiscal year, I'll practically be able to pay this stuff out of petty cash."

She rests her cheek against the top of my head.

"It will be a loan, of course," I tell her. "Timmy Failure doesn't give handouts."

She wraps both her arms around my chest and squeezes me into hers.

"But when the agency expands, we'll most likely have a position for you, and we'll just deduct the funds owed from your paycheck."

She blows really hard into my ear. It's something she does sometimes because it makes me laugh.

"Be professional," I tell her.

She stops.

"Do it again," I say.

CHAPTER 20

Bean There, Done That

I am climbing Rollo Tookus's dresser to show him how the monkeys put the toilet paper in the Webers' tree.

He is barely paying attention.

"Sorry. Our English test is in four days. I can't focus."

So I tell him about Garbanzo Man.

"Who's Garbanzo Man?"

"He's the agency's new mascot. I built him out of old clothes and a paper bag, all of which I stuffed with newspapers." I show him a snapshot I keep in my pocket.

"What's the point?" asks Rollo.

"He's meant to convey a sense of fearsome greatness. I want to really intimidate the idiot that stole the Failuremobile. Intimidate the person so much that they give it back. I'm going to put him on our front lawn next to a big sign that says, GARBANZO MAN SEES ALL."

"That doesn't make any sense."

"You don't make any sense. You're not focused," I tell him. "Besides, you know nothing about marketing."

"Why'd you name him Garbanzo Man?"

"Because *garbanzo* means big."

"You're thinking of *giganto*. Garbanzo is a bean."

That's the thing about guys like Rollo Tookus. They think they know everything, but they don't.

"Anyhow, I have to study," Rollo says. "I've got my tutor coming over to help me in a half hour."

This is where I should tell you about the little fly in the ointment of my friendship with Rollo Tookus. Actually it's not a little fly. It's a garbanzo fly.

And it looks like this:

That's right. Rollo Tookus's tutor is none other than the Beast. And I don't want to rehash the umpteen arguments this has caused, so I'll just sum up our respective positions.

Rollo's Position: Corrina Corrina is really smart and helps him get A's.

Timmy's Position: Rollo is a big, stupid traitor.

Now, in fairness, I will say that when Rollo is around me, he tries not to say her name. He just says "tutor." And he gives me plenty of warning before she comes over, so I don't have to be in the same room with someone so unethical.

"All right, Rollo, I'm out of here. But do me a favor. Be on the lookout for clues. I think your tutor may have committed grand theft auto."

"What are you talking about?"

"I think she stole the Failuremobile."

Rollo closes his book and stares at me. "Her dad is rich, Timmy. I don't think she needs your Failuremobile."

"This isn't about what *she* needs, Rollo! It's what *I* need. And I need the Failuremobile. Don't you recognize industrial sabotage when you see it?"

"Listen, Timmy. I really have to study. If you're so sure she took it, why don't you pay a surprise visit to that bank where she has her office? See if it's there."

I have to admit it was the one decent tip Rollo's ever given me, so I drop a quarter in his pencil cup and pat him on the head.

I show myself out and walk down the gritty streets. Streets strewn with crumpled newspapers.

A whole lot of crumpled newspapers.

A trail of which leads to my front lawn.

And to the remnants of a man who was not as fearsome and garbanzo as I thought.

CHAPTER 21
You Can Always Go Downtown

I head downtown to do reconnaissance on CCIA headquarters. Because I am so well known and don't want to draw attention to myself, I go undercover.

Under my bed cover.

Even so, I hate to miss an opportunity to promote, so I use the back of the blanket.

Unfortunately the disguise does not help. And I am hounded by admirers.

But I do not mind. For on these downtown streets, I sense it.

The whole world has changed.

Changed because in the shadow of the future home of Total Failure, Inc., I see my destiny.

A destiny with which no man can tinker.

I am the soon-to-be head of the world's largest detective agency.

A multibillion-dollar employer of thousands who made it big by adhering to one simple credo: Greatness.

I am a detective without peer.

A visionary without limits.

A pioneer of tomorrow whose only challenge now is to remain humble.

So for now, I walk humbly down the sidewalk to the pathetic bank that is CCIA's headquarters, all to follow up on Rollo's tip about the Failuremobile. A tip that will prove to be wrong. Because Rollo Tookus is always wrong.

But that is okay.

Because the tip has brought me here.

To the site of my skyscraper of greatness.

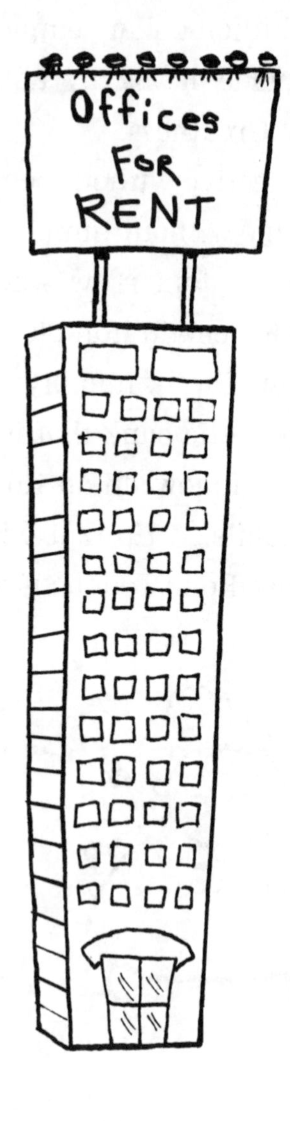

Which is right next door to the bank.

Behind which is something I recognize.

The whole world has changed.

CHAPTER 22

Happiness Is Not a Dumb Blanket

Here's how this chapter should have gone:

Timmy Failure runs to the back of the bank. He seizes the Failuremobile. The Evil One bursts out of the bank's front door. Timmy seizes her by the collar of her evil coat.

"I have caught you, Evil One."

The Evil One shrieks.

"Your shrieks will avail you not," Timmy declares, "for you have been caught red-handed."

The Evil One cries.

"Your tears will avail you not," Timmy declares, "for you are history. As is your agency. It is all over. You are through."

Head down, hands cuffed behind her evil back, the Evil One calls out to Timmy as she is escorted to the police van.

"What do you want, Evil One?" asks a gracious Timmy.

"To tell you one thing," she replies, drooling with envy from one corner of her sad little mouth.

"Say it," Timmy commands.

"You are greatness personified," she says.

But that is not how this chapter will go. Because before all that could happen, this did:

That's right. The United States government stopped me by snagging a corner of my bed cover on one of their mailboxes. Why?

A bribe.

By whom?

Her nickname rhymes with the Weevil Bun.

Let me just say this: It's a sad day when the government of the people, by the people, and for the people decides to affix those people to mailboxes.

But affix me they did.

And trapped I was.

Until twenty minutes later, when I realized I could take the blanket off my head.

Only to see I was too late.

For the Failuremobile was gone.

Surely whisked off by the same government officials who affixed me to the mailbox.

But okay. Now I knew the odds. Me against

the Weevil Bun and all the governments of the world. Daunting for most. But I am not most. I am Timmy Failure. And no person or government or force of nature can stop me.

Except maybe being cold at night because I forgot to retrieve my blanket and can't depend on a "friend" to share his.

CHAPTER 23

The Timmynator's Judgment Day

Surrounded by dingoes.

Buried alive.

Doing math.

These are just three of the horrific places I'd rather be than the place I currently am.

Which is standing next to the Furious Rage that is my mother in the garage.

"Where is it, Timmy?" she shouts. "Where is my Segway?"

"What are you doing out here?" I answer.

"Cleaning out the garage," she says. "And I want to know where that Segway is!"

"Why are you cleaning out the garage?"

"Timmy, tell me where that Segway is!"

My left eye twitches. Then my right. It is something that happens when I'm nervous.

"I don't know."

She says nothing.

I say nothing.

And it is then that I see the fury disappear from her eyes. Replaced by something worse. Something I cannot surmount.

Mom tears.

I shout out the first desperate thing that pops into my large brain. "Molly Moskins needed it for a play!"

This stuns my mother *and* me.

"Who's Molly Moskins?" she asks, wiping the corner of one eye.

"An annoying girl who smells like a tangerine," I want to say.

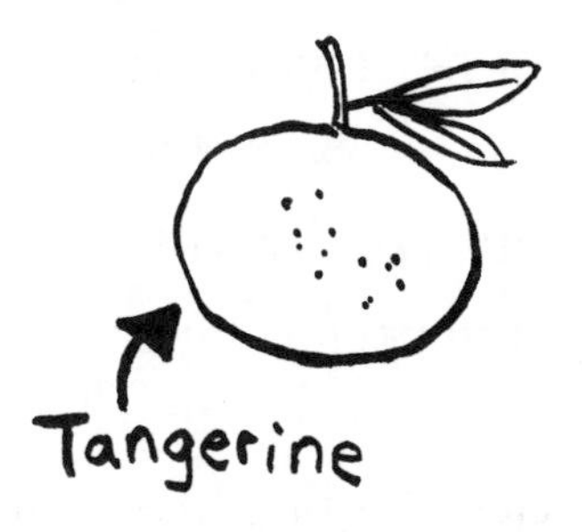

But I don't say that. I say this: "A girl in my class. She's putting on a school play. And the main character drives a Segway. Don't ask me. It's her lousy play."

My mother pauses, her frustration subsiding. "Well, you should have asked, because it wasn't yours to loan."

"I know," I tell her. "Mistakes were made."

"Well, when can she return it?"

"Next week," I blurt out, "when the play is over."

Stupid me. I should have said next month. Bought more time. Those mom tears have clouded my judgment.

"Fine. But it better be returned *that day*."

I saunter out of the garage. Trying to avert suspicion. Give my mom a quick wave. Dumb move. I never wave. Get it together, man.

Once out of her sight, I run for it. I know that I have to get to Molly Moskins before she does. Get our stories straight.

Granted, my performance wasn't pretty. But it worked.

And at least it adhered to my brilliantly conceived plan concerning the missing Failuremobile.

CHAPTER 24

The Furry Burrito

I do not like Señor Burrito.

She is Molly Moskins's cat. And every time I turn my head, she dunks her paw into my tea.

"She likes you!" says Molly Moskins. "That's how she shows it!"

I am tolerating this because I need Molly Moskins. Need her to corroborate my lie. So I am on her porch, and we are having a tea party.

"We should have a tea party once a week! It would be wondermarvelously splendiferous!" shouts Molly, displaying her tendency to use words that do not exist. She has been so excited from the moment I showed up at her door that she has not stopped yapping. I have not even had the chance to tell her that her female cat is a Señora and not a Señor.

"Molly, we need to talk about something."

"Oh, I love to talk," she says, pointing at my hat. "Do you like biscuits?"

I turn to face her, staring directly into those bizarrely mismatched pupils.

"Molly Moskins, my agency needs you."

"Ooooh," she says. "A modeling agency? You probably want me for my eyes."

"No, Molly," I explain, "it's not a modeling agency. It's a *detective* agency."

As I say this, I hear a *sploosh.*

It is Señor Burrito.

And she has taken advantage of my head turn to dunk *two* paws into my tea.

"Molly, my agency solves major international crimes. It is on the verge of being a multibillion-dollar corporation. The largest of its kind."

I let that sink in. Her mismatched eyes widen. "I *love* biscuits!" she says, pointing at my hat again.

I stand up to leave. "You're wasting my resources, Molly. And I have cases to solve. I'll show myself out."

But before I can walk down the porch steps, she rushes to block my way. The sudden movement sends tangerine smell everywhere. "Don't leave!" shouts the Tangerine Girl. "I have cases! Lots of cases!"

She grabs my hand and runs inside toward her bedroom, where she slides open her closet door.

"My shoes are missing!"

Behind her is a large shoe organizer. It is filled with dozens of shoes.

"Well, not *all* of them are missing. But many of them. Someone international stole them!"

Finally. An international case.

I return to the porch table to take copious notes. The first of which is this:

Do not leave Señor Burrito unattended.

CHAPTER 25

No Jet for You

You cannot rent an F-16 fighter jet.

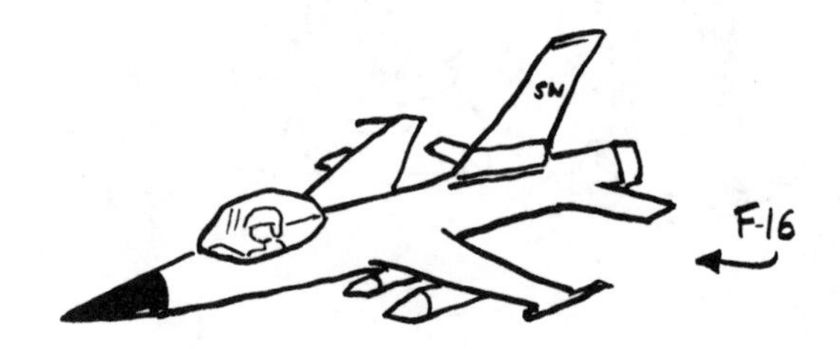

At least that's what they'll tell you if you and your polar bear walk into an army recruiting center. Nor will they give you a Chinook helicopter.

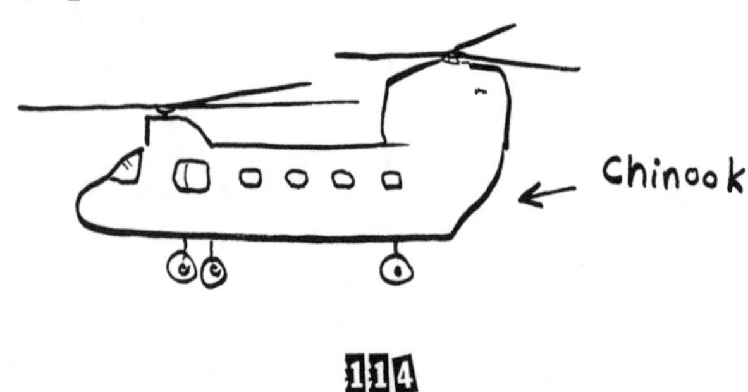

I explain that I am only going to level a bank. Not even a classy one.

"I can give you this," the army recruiter says, pointing to the water cooler and handing me a Dixie cup.

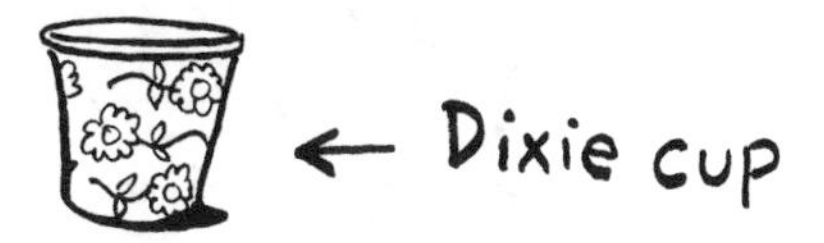

Total licks his lips.

"Sir, it appears you don't understand," I tell him. "I've declared all-out war against the Evil One."

He looks up from his paperwork. I stare back at him. "She's a four-foot-tall menace to society."

He rubs his eyes. "Listen, son. I've got work to do. If you're interested in joining the army, come see me when you're eighteen."

What did I expect from the same government officials who affixed me to the mailbox?

God knows what the Evil One has told them about me. The lies, the defamatory statements.

Surely she has attempted to frame me as a loon.

Which is why I wore the shirt I wore to the recruiting center that day.

Sadly, my business partner took no such steps to ensure that he, too, made a good first impression. I tried to explain to him that this was the army. An army with rigorous weight requirements.

And that he didn't fit them.

But no. The big guy refused to lose weight. So when we walked into the recruiting office to rent a fighter jet—*wham*—we made a sloppy first impression. Just like I told him we would.

I think when my all-out war with the Weevil Bun is over, I'll do the poor mammal a favor. Like send him to business school. Maybe there they'll teach him what a Dixie cup is.

And maybe the next time we walk into an army recruiting center, we won't get kicked out again for doing this:

CHAPTER 26

Late-Night Epiphanies of the Sole

I wake at three a.m.

With a revelation.

(These things happen to good detectives. Our large brains never stop.)

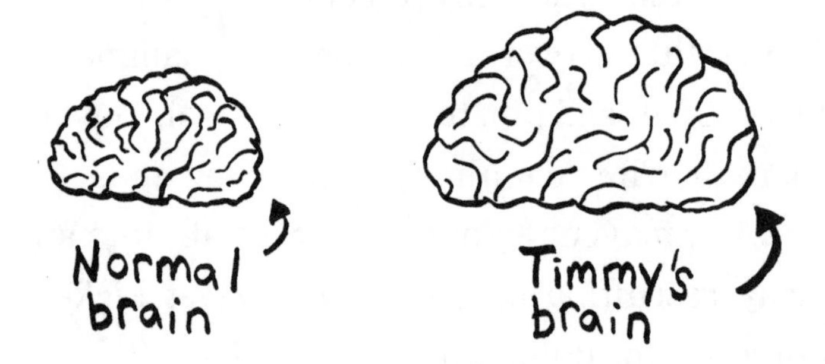

And that revelation was this:

When I was with Molly Moskins and told her I was going to leave her house because I was a very busy detective, she stopped me and asked me to stay, suddenly claiming that many of her shoes had been stolen. I asked her to identify one of the stolen shoes. She pointed to a red shoe in her closet and said the other one was missing.

But she was hiding it behind her back.

That's when it hits me. What she was up to.

So I make a note of it in my detective log.

CHAPTER 27

Grabbing the Bull by the Horns

Something is wrong with our educational system.

I say that because it is boring.

If educators really wanted us to learn, they would include little things during the school day that would make learning more interesting.

For example, put Rollo Tookus and a bull in an enclosed space.

That would teach me to never play with bulls. Instead, Rollo Tookus is my study partner. And he's dull as sand.

The way this whole study partner thing works is that the teacher pairs you with someone else in the class. You teach the lesson to him. He teaches the lesson to you.

Today's lesson is about identifying conjunctions. Here's how Rollo teaches me.

Here's how I teach Rollo.

"Knock it off," Rollo says. "Crocus will see us."

"No, he won't," I tell him. "He's reading Key West brochures at his desk."

"What for?"

"Who knows? Listen. I need your help."

"With what?"

"You need to infiltrate the CCIA."

"Infiltrate what?" he asks.

Old Man Crocus raises the tips of his eyeglasses above his vacation brochures. "Do you two not have enough to do?"

"We do, Mr. Crocus," Rollo says. What a butt kisser.

I lower my voice. "It's Corrina Corrina's intelligence agency. She's got my Failure-mobile. I saw it there myself."

"Shhhh," Rollo says quietly. "I don't want anything to do with your stupid plans."

"Okay," I tell him. "That's fine."

"Good," he says.

"But I think the next test is another group test," I tell him. "Hope I can do as well as I did the last time."

Rollo's head starts to shake like a maraca.

"Fine!" he says. "I'll do it. Now are we done?"

So I add one more thing.

"How do you feel about bulls?"

CHAPTER 28

Home at Safe

"You look fine," I tell Rollo.

"I do not look fine. I look stupid."

He is dressed as a Shasta daisy.

"How is this supposed to get me into Corrina Corrina's bank?" he asks.

"We've gone over this."

"Say it again."

"You're Dickie the Daisy. You're part of the Human Flower Parade."

Artist's Rendering of what Human Flower Parade Might Look Like

"So why am I stopping at a bank?"

"Because Dickie the Daisy wants to open an account."

"But she's just gonna say it's no longer a bank. It's the CC-whatever."

"Doesn't matter. By that time, you're done looking around. Scoping the place out."

"Why don't I just go as myself?"

"Too suspicious. She knows we're friends."

I hand him four quarters. "What's this for?" he asks.

"Bus fare. You can't ride the Totalmobile. You'd blow your cover."

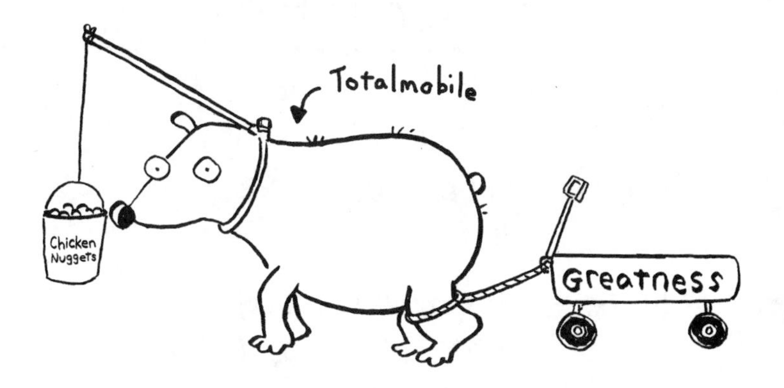

"I can't do this."

"You'll be fine."

But no. He would not be fine. He would be Rollo.

What follows next is so aggravating to my professional sensibilities that I hesitate to include it in this book. It demonstrates how even a brilliantly conceived plan such as this can be decimated by the bumblings of a moronic amateur. To distance myself from it, I have made Rollo write it in his own hand.

MY ACCOUNT

BY ROLLO TOOKUS

2:55 PM — ATTEMPTED TO BOARD BUS.

2:56 PM — BUS DRIVER YELLS, "HEY, WEIRDO, GET OFF MY BUS."

2:57 PM — BEGIN LONG WALK TO BANK.

2:59 PM — DAISY PETALS POKING PEOPLE IN EYE. PEOPLE MAD.

3:01 PM — ANGRY MAN WITH HURT EYE STARTS PLUCKING OUT MY PETALS.

3:04 PM —

4:30 PM — ARRIVE AT BANK.

KNOCK ON DOOR.

CORRINA CORRINA SAYS,

"WHO ARE YOU?"

I SAY — "DICKIE THE DAISY."

SHE SAYS I LOOK LIKE A SAD BUNNY.

I TELL HER, "I'M DICKIE THE SAD BUNNY." SHE SAYS,

"WHAT THE HECK IS GOING ON HERE?"

4:31 PM — ~~[illegible]~~ MY HEAD STARTS SHAKING.
CORRINA CORRINA SAYS, "IS THAT YOU, ROLLO?"
I SAY, "NO, CORRINA CORRINA."
~~[illegible]~~

4:32 PM — COVER BLOWN
CORRINA CORRINA SAYS,
"COME INSIDE, ROLLO.
TELL ME WHAT'S GOING ON."
TOTAL PANIC NOW.
I SAY, "BIG PARADE.
ME DICKIE. DICKIE WANT
OPEN BANK!"

4:34 PM — ~~[illegible]~~

CORRINA CORRINA CONCERNED FOR MY HEALTH. HEAD WON'T STOP SHAKING.

CORRINA CORRINA OFFERS ME A GLASS OF WATER. I SAY,

"WATER NO.
ME NEED
LEAVE!"

CAN'T SPEAK.

CORRINA CORRINA RECEIVES PHONE CALL. WALKS OUT OF ROOM.

I TRY TO DO MISSION.

CHECK OUT PLACE.

FIND GIANT ROOM

WHERE BANK KEEPS SAFE.

WALK INSIDE.

HEAR SOUND OF

GIANT STEEL DOOR

BEING CLOSED.

PAGE 6

4:35 PM TO 8:30 AM: Locked in Safe

I really don't want to go into all the stuff Rollo did during that long night:

- Hyperventilating when he phoned me on his little emergency cell phone
- Calling me unfortunate names
- Not saying thank you when I called his mom for him and lied, saying Rollo was spending the night at my house
- Not listening attentively as I read him my copyrighted work "Surviving Enemy Capture on Beans and a Smile"

- Scaring the poor janitor who came to clean the bank that morning, only to find a mutant bunny

The only regret I have from that night is the inadequate job Rollo did regarding reconnaissance. Because when I asked him for a blueprint of the bank, I expected more than this:

CHAPTER 29

Movin' On Up

So here's why my mom was cleaning out the garage:

We're moving.

She says that with all the stuff going on with her work, we have to move into an apartment.

All of this is neither here nor there because we will soon be making more money than is decent.

But the short-term effect is that Total Failure, Inc., will finally be freed from the degradingly small closet in which it is currently confined. And that can only boost workplace morale.

I've scheduled a teleconference with my mother to discuss the new office space I'll have in the apartment. I've even submitted a design schematic for how the apartment should be laid out.

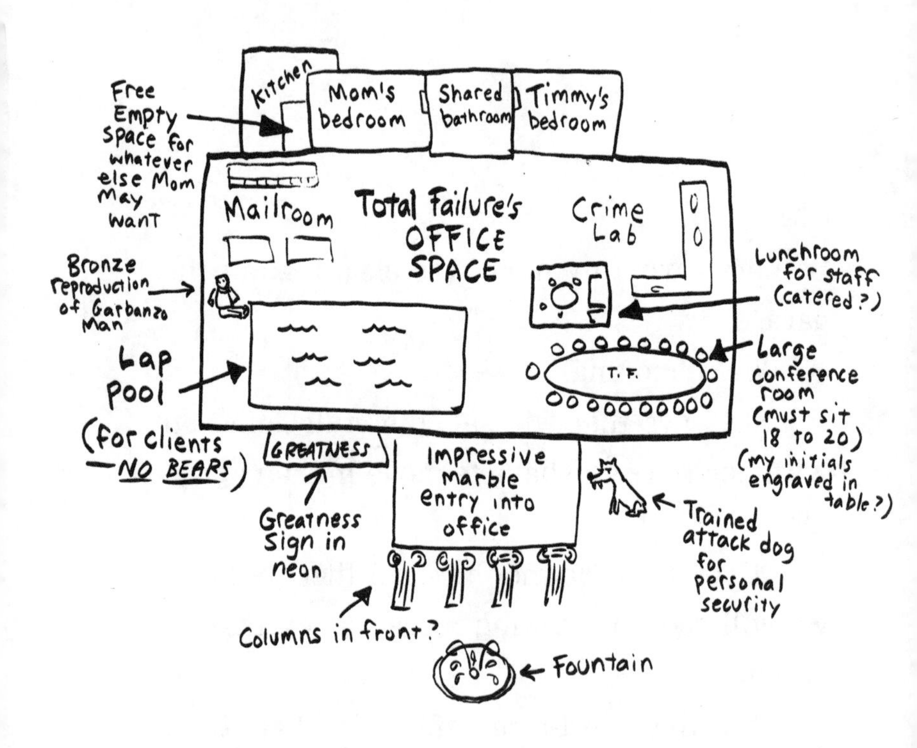

In a further upswing of good fortune, I've solved the Weber case.

Perhaps you recall it. If not, look here.

I focused all of my resources on it in order to show the Weevil Bun that I am not a detective to be trifled with.

How did I solve it?

Clue No. 1: Jimmy Weber said it was not the first "TP" job his family had seen. *TP* stands for "tiny person." And who's a tiny person?

Besides, we already know Molly Moskins is an international shoe thief. That's called recidivism (i.e., a tendency to relapse into criminal behavior).

But the biggest clue of all was the second one. One that I stumbled upon quite accidentally.

You may recall that while at Molly Moskins's house, I drank a fair amount of tea (at least before Señor Burrito sat in it). As a result, I needed to use the facilities.

And that's where I saw it. Hanging for all to see.

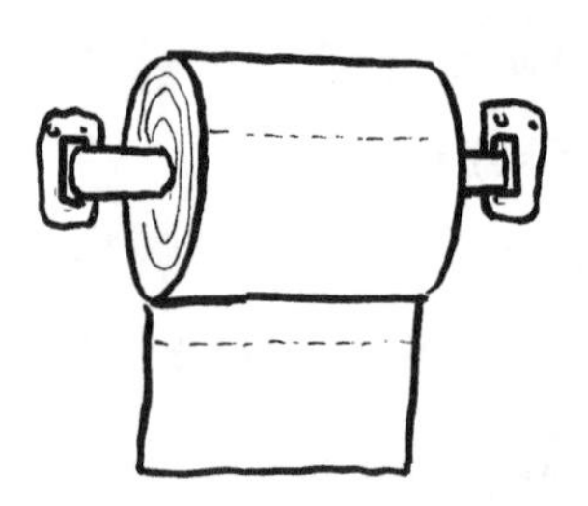

That's right. Toilet paper. The weapon of choice for the Webers' attacker.

In the bathroom of Molly Moskins.

The girl's on one heck of a crime spree.

CHAPTER 30

The Chute Heard Round the World

Clang kong ding a bing ding dong.

Is not a new song.

It is the sound the trash makes as it falls down the chute in our new apartment building. I am familiar with it because it is directly adjacent to Total Failure's world headquarters.

In the hallway.

That's right. Ignoring my repeated requests for a teleconference, my mother rented a tiny one-bedroom apartment. Now I sleep on a fold-out couch in the den.

And my corporate headquarters is by the trash chute in the apartment building's hallway.

Normally I'd call a board meeting to discuss this untenable arrangement. But I can't. Because I do not have the support of half the board.

That half is happier than ever.

CHAPTER 31

Ebb and Flo

Deep in the rat-infested bowels of the earth.

At the end of a maze of torchlit tunnels.

Guarded by attack dogs.

Is where the Failuremobile is.

I don't know that for sure. But it's my detective's instinct. Which is rarely wrong.

And those bowels are most likely located below CCIA headquarters. Although I can't yet confirm that either. Because someone was a bad daisy.

Seizing the vehicle from the vicious dogs is a natural job for Total. He is the top of the Arctic food chain. But the last time I saw Total interact with a dog, he did this:

That's the problem with an Arctic predator like Total. You give him a seal and *wham*—he's got lunch. But you give him a dog and *wham*—he's got companionship.

To give Total better odds of seizing the Failuremobile, I've begun sending letters to the Weevil Bun. Letters containing subliminal messages.

But for some reason, all the letters have come back stamped UNDELIVERABLE. Maybe it's how I'm addressing them.

Those aren't the only letters I'm having trouble delivering. Lately all my complaints to the Better Detective Bureau have also been getting kicked back to me. Like this one I filed after the Rollo bank incident:

I suspect from all this that the United States Postal Service is in the back pocket of the Weevil Bun. First they affix me to a mailbox. Now they block my mail.

Unable to rely on the postal service, I have decided to embrace technology.

The cost was higher than anticipated.

Thus, I scheduled a teleconference with my mother. Here are the minutes:

Fortunately I have options. Like my local library. And that is where Flo the Librarian comes in.

Meet Flo.

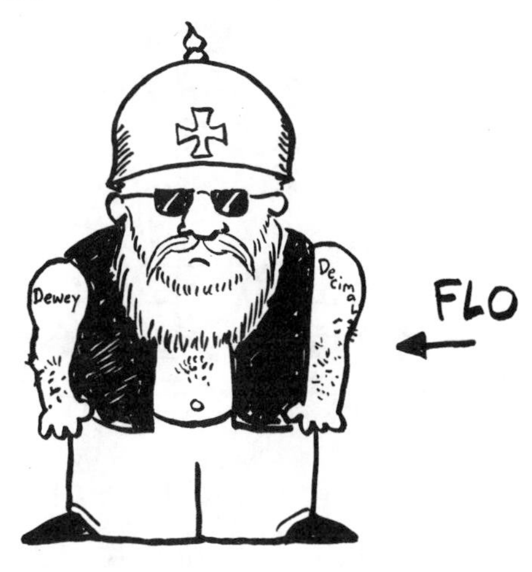

CHAPTER 32

Emily the Fist

You do not want to exceed the twenty-minute maximum for Internet use at my library. Because if you do, you see this:

That's an unhappy Flo. And *Flo* is not short for *Florence.* It's short for "Misshelve my books and the blood may FLOw."

I've never actually seen Flo the Librarian pummel anyone. But there've been rumors. Rumors of users wandering into the stacks and not returning. Fingers lost in card-catalog drawers.

So people do not misshelve books at my library. They do not tear pages out of magazines. And they do not ask stupid questions.

This arrangement works for me because Flo and I are professional colleagues. For example, he knows I have connections. Connections that if need be could one day spring him from the clink. The pokey. The big house.

The Big House

And I, in turn, know he's looking out for the Timmynator. For example, say I want to go over the twenty-minute time allotment for Internet usage. I just give him a look. And he gives me a grunt.

Professional Colleagues

Sure, it's a special privilege. Something not available to the common man. But that's the way the seamy underbelly of detective work is. Looks are traded. Bodies disappear.

Internet time limits are exceeded.

And Internet time is what I need right now. Because I'm building a website.

Well, *I'm* not. Flo is.

He saw me trying to do it myself and grunted. So I got up. And he sat down. And he started pounding on the keys with his big chubby fingers.

I told him I wanted the first screen to say this:

Then the second screen to say this:

And the third screen to say this:

And the fourth screen to say this:

But Flo did something wrong. And now when you log on to the site, you see this:

I'd say something to Flo about it, but I need to pick the right moment. And those are scarce. Scarce because when Flo sits behind his librarian's desk, he reads. And Flo does not like to be disturbed. Word is he reads books on how to kill things. And how to dispose of dead bodies. And how to crush things with your fist. I actually saw one of the books once. It had an odd title:

I'm assuming it's titled that because this Emily woman has written multiple books on crushing things with your fist. But then I looked her up on the Internet.

And if she can crush things with her fist, her photo is somewhat misleading.

EMILY DICKINSON
Crusher of Things with
Her Fist

CHAPTER 33

Milking Technology for All It's Worth

My World Wide Web site is not the only way I am changing the course of history. I am using the library's computers to send electronic mail. Or, as some in the detective industry like to term it, "e-mail."[1]

Electronic mail and World Wide Web sites are all part of my multipronged strategy to grow the business and destroy the Corrina. I obtained the Weevil Bun's electronic mail address from a flyer she posted in the library.

1. Do not attempt to memorize all these industry terms. They are highly technical. I have written the narrative in such a way that terms like this can be contextually understood by the average reader.

The flyer was defamatory.

The defamatory nature of the flyer is the subject of an electronic-mail complaint I have sent to the Better Detective Bureau.

To: BetterDetectiveBureau@geemails.com
From: TimmyFailure@yahoos.com
Subject: Defamation

I am inferior to no one.

I am also sending bogus electronic mails directly to the Weevil Bun herself. The purpose of these communications is to provide her with false leads. Waste her agency's resources. Send her on futile searches. Here is one I sent yesterday:

To: CorrinaCorrina@geemails.com

I am a cow that may have witnessed a murder.

Please find me so we can talk.

P.S. If it helps, I go, "Moooooo."

Too bad the library's scanner was not working.

Otherwise, I would have included this helpful map:

I am somewhere around here.

CHAPTER 34
Zero, My Hero

Some say the zero was invented by the Mayans. They say it was a big deal. I do not know why. But I do know that without it, you could not write this score:

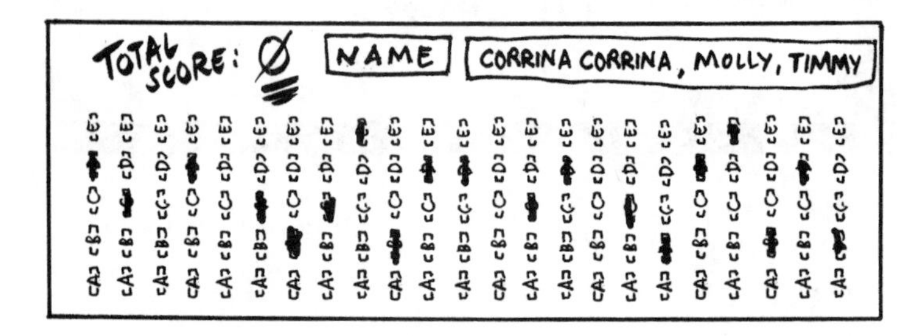

That's our group English test. The one Rollo was worried about.

(Well, the most *recent* one he was worried about, anyway.)

But he was out sick. So that left just me,

Molly, and the Weevil Bun. And our teamwork was not ideal.

That left the Weevil Bun to answer all of the questions herself. So she did. And through dumb luck, she got them all right. But I could not share answers with a moral degenerate. So after she turned in the test, I grabbed it and changed all the answers. *A*'s became *B*'s. *B*'s became *C*'s. *C*'s became *D*'s.

And our A became an F.

That was too much for the Weevil Bun. So she complained. Said she no longer wanted to be in a group. And here's how Old Man Crocus responded.

The man is crumbling. I don't know what part of the educational system finally did him in, but I do have an educated guess.

That guess is about the only part of me that *is* educated right now. Because Crocus has given up. No more parent-teacher conferences. No more calling me Captain Thickhead. No more putting me with the smart kids. Now he just sits at his desk reading travel guides. Sometimes in a palm-tree shirt.

And when that doesn't work, he pulls out a little hula-girl statue and watches her hula.

He doesn't even seem to be bothered by the moral stand I took against the degenerate Weevil Bun on the latest group test. Though he does seem to resent one thing.

My fans.

CHAPTER 35

Raisin Heck

When a bowler gets three strikes in a row, it is called a turkey. Here is another bowling turkey:

His name is Crispin Flavius. And here is everything I know about him:

1. He bowls.
2. He is dating my mother.
3. I call him "the bowling turkey."

I met him yesterday. He was sitting at my dinner table eating raisins. So I guess I know a fourth thing about him:

4. He eats raisins.

I should say here that I loathe raisins. Though that did not stop me from initiating a friendly dialogue.

My mother said they met somewhere. And then she said something else. But I didn't hear any of it because it was then that I noticed the bowling turkey's upturned collar. So I tried to help.

Then I noticed something growing under his lower lip.

Then I noticed he only had one earring.

Disturbed by our exchange, I retreated to the bathroom to record an accurate assessment of him in my detective log.

When I returned to the dinner table, I was met with silence. I looked at my mother. "Crispin would like it if you'd take your hat off for dinner," she said.

"Gentlemen don't wear hats to dinner," he added.

I responded as best I could.

That was not received well. So my mother sent me to my room. But I don't have a room. I have a foldout couch.

So I took Total and went to Rollo's house. Where I was not received well either.

CHAPTER 36

Eureka

There's no point trying to explain a principled stand to Rollo. So the next time I see him, I bring him a gift.

To further lift his spirits, I bring up the Molly Moskins case. I don't really want his input. But it makes him feel good.

"I can't do this right now, Timmy. You've ruined my GPA."

“So you think I should arrest her?”

“I think I need to study.”

“If I don’t, no shoe is safe. And God knows what she’ll do with toilet paper.”

Rollo closes his book and turns to look at me. “If I tell you what I think is happening, will you let me study?”

I lock my hands behind my head and laugh. “Okay, big guy, shoot.”

“Molly Moskins likes you. She wants you to spend time with her. So she hides her own shoes and pretends that they’re stolen.”

I laugh so hard I have trouble catching my breath.

“Sorry about that,” I tell him. “It’s just hard sometimes to listen to the musings of amateurs.”

“Fine. I told you what I think. Now can you go? I have ten minutes before I have to go meet my tutor.”

"I thought the Weevil Bun came here," I say.

"It's not for tutoring. She left something last time she was here. I told her I'd return it."

"Then let me follow you. Knowing where she lives is vital intelligence."

"*I* don't even know where she lives," he says. "I'm meeting her at a coffee shop."

"You're a traitor and a fiend," I tell him. "So what did she leave?"

"Her backpack," he says.

I look at the backpack. It has an aura of badness.

"You should burn it to cleanse the room," I tell him.

"I'm going to the bathroom," he says. "When I come back, can you please be gone?"

So he walks out.

Leaving me with the backpack.

I don't want to rifle through it. But it's obvious that Rollo's departure is a subtle signal for me to do just that.

So I do what he wants me to do and look through it.

And all I find are stupid schoolbooks and pencil cases and scarves (oh, trying to be like me?).

Until I get to the last pocket.

And find the Holy Grail.

CHAPTER 37

Da Corrina Code

With no privacy to be had in my trash-chute office, I rush to the library with the enemy's secrets. I run in a crooked line to avoid assassins.

I enter the library. Nod to Flo. He clears a cubicle. I check for bombs.

I post Total at the rear entrance. Protection for my exposed flank.

Perimeter secured, I begin reading the log. Which, to demonstrate my fairness, I present to you here without comment.

Other than the comments I've written all over the attached sticky notes.

Monday, October 16

Tonight I sit in my room alone. Dad still at work. Nanny watching T.V. I go to bed before Dad gets home.

↑ Likely story. Probably
stealing

Tuesday, October 17

I wake up. Nanny says Dad left early. Big box for me on the breakfast table. Inside is a pair of binoculars. Card says, "To help you with your next case. Love, Dad."

Dad right. ↗

Thursday, October 19

Jimmy Weber offers me case. I accept as favor to him.

↑ GROSS distortion of truth FILE STOLEN ILLEGAL

Friday, October 20

I solve Weber case when I overhear Chris Thompkins brag he TP'ed the Webers.

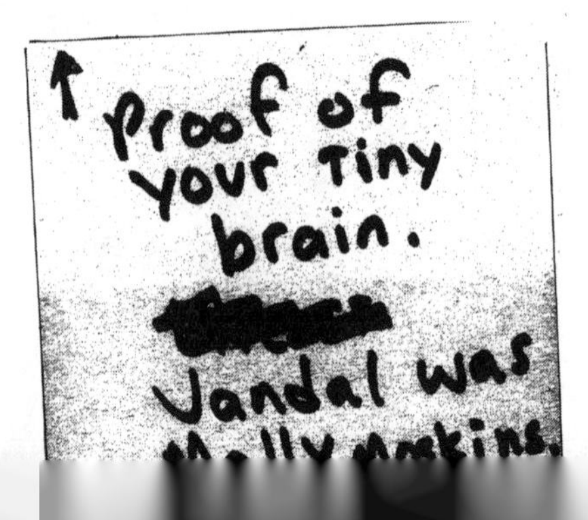

Wednesday, October 25
I finish casework early
to have movie night
with Dad.
Admission
of poor
work
ethic.

Thursday, October 26

Movie night cancelled.
Dad had business trip.

Jimmy Weber pays me for solving TP case. I tell him I don't deserve it for so little work. I give money back.

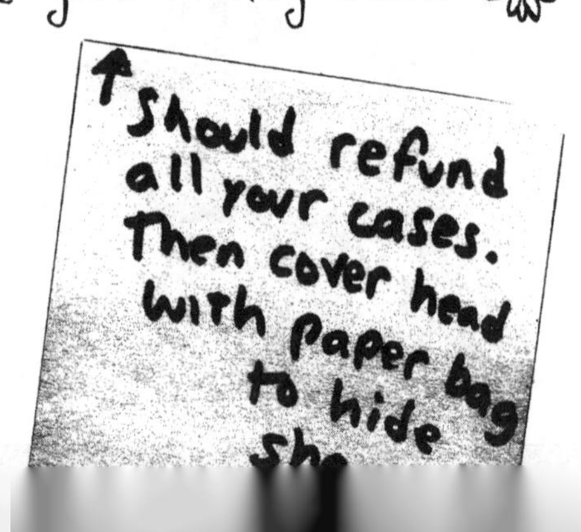

I search the entire log for references to me.

But there are none.

The closest I can find is a reference to Rollo.

The weird kid in our group makes us all fail the test.

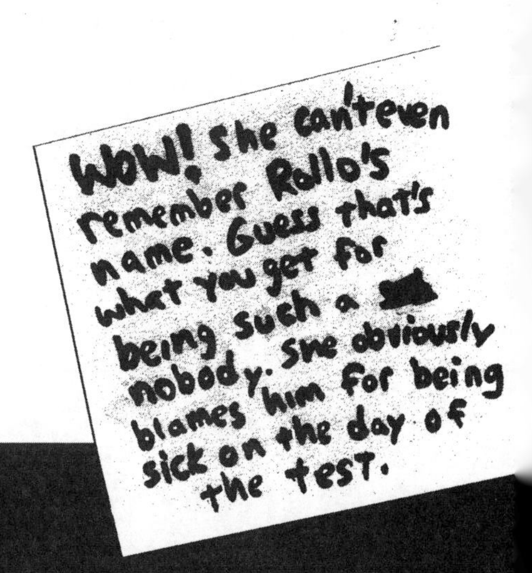

And that's when it hits me. What this log really is.

A plant.

No, not that kind of plant. A scheme. A ruse. A setup. To wit: All detectives know that when a company wants to hide its dirty secrets, it keeps two sets of books. The sanitized one they want the police to see. And the real one.

Knowing I'd go to Rollo's house, she purposely planted the sanitized one in her backpack in the hopes that I'd read it and see no references to me. Then I'd conclude she had nothing to do with the theft of the Failuremobile!

So now I just need to find the real one. The one that looks like this:

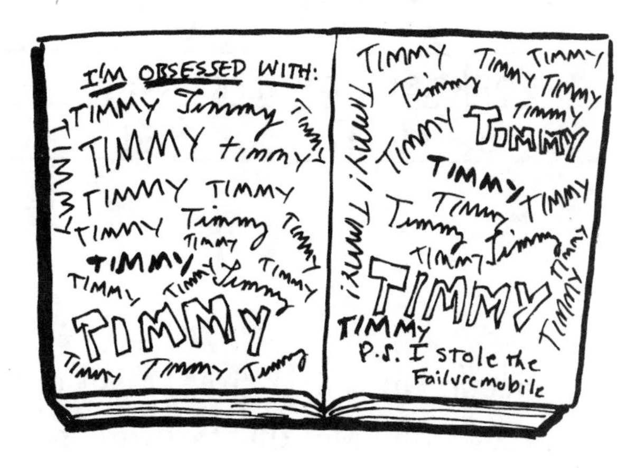

CHAPTER 38

Darkness on the Edge of My Foldout Bed

I am awakened by sniper fire. I rush to look outside. It is Molly Moskins throwing pebbles against my window.

"What do you want?" I ask.

"I was thinking we should practice the play," she says.

Earlier that day, I had brought Molly Moskins to my office to discuss the play. Now she knows where I live.

"Go away, Molly Moskins. The play's not real. I explained that."

"We should probably practice anyway," she says.

"This is not a good time, Molly Moskins. I am in possession of classified information. I cannot be standing in front of an open window." I slam the window shut and return to my foldout bed.

A clump of dirt cracks the windowpane. "What now?" I cry, rushing back to the window. "You have caused grievous property damage."

"My shoes have been stolen!" she shouts. "Internationally stolen!"

It is true. She is now in her socks.

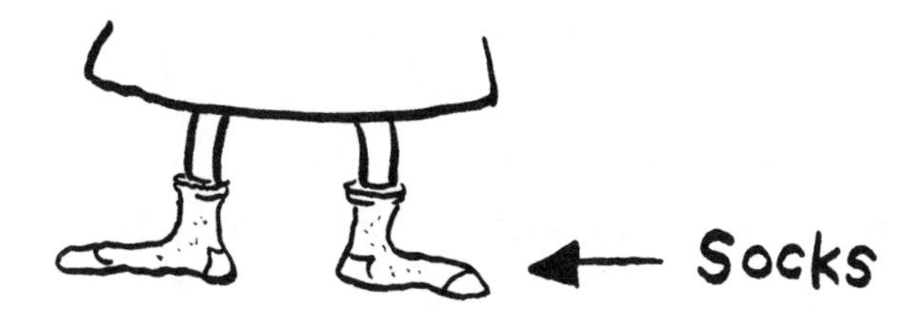

I grab my detective log. I make a note to open a file in the morning.

And that's when I realize she is holding something behind her back.

And that's when I figure it out. First she had on shoes. Now she does not. And now she is holding something behind her back.

I make a sketch of what I know is in her hands.

"Drop it right now, Molly Moskins!" I shout. "We shall not be victimized by your spree!"

My mother swings open her bedroom door and turns on the living-room light. "Why are you yelling?" she asks.

She sees me standing in front of the window. The broken one. "And how did that happen?" she yells.

"We were the victim of a criminal mastermind," I tell her. "Be thankful. It could have been much worse."

"What are you talking about?" she asks.

"The little terror was going to tiptoe around in her socks. It's called *stealth*."

"Who?" she yells.

I point out the window. We see only bushes.

"Timmy, I had to put down a huge security deposit for this place. And you know what happens with something like this? It comes right out of that deposit."

She is incredibly unappreciative.

"First you loan out my Segway for some play without asking. Then you break the window. When are you going to learn to respect other people's property?"

I withstand the barrage in silence. I am a genius unrecognized in his own home.

"And by the way," she adds, putting her hands on her hips, "I had a little talk with your friend Rollo Tookus yesterday."

Wonderful, I thought. No good can come of this.

"He came over looking for something he said was missing from a backpack. So I asked him about this little school play."

My left eye twitches. Then my right.

"And you know what he said?" she asks.

I don't. But I am rooting for the rotund kid like never before.

"He said there wasn't one."

Subterfuge! Betrayal! I hop on my foldout bed and shout:

My speech is bold. Defiant. Even stirring. But then I add this:

Saturday. As in the day three days from Wednesday. Wednesday being today. It is a lie so profound and far reaching that I want to modify the bottom of my left shoe.

My mother smiles and turns off the light. And answers me from the dark.

"I'd like that very much."

CHAPTER 39

I Need Paw

We are going to storm the castle. The castle being this:

The stormer being this:

We have no time to waste. Total will smash in the door. Rise on his hind legs. And roar with an Arctic fury that makes seals weep. One thousand, five hundred furious pounds. All demanding the Failuremobile.

In polar-bear-ese.

Which may require translation.

The sign was my idea. The wording was Total's.

I didn't like it. So I nixed it for something more primeval. More beastly. More Frankenstein.

Sure, the sign lost clarity. But now it was direct. Intimidating.

My plan was to accompany my business partner to the bank. Guard the exits. But I can't.

Because I'm trapped.

In the bowling turkey's shiny Cadillac.

I am being held hostage against my will. Or, as my mother describes it, I am going to the hardware store. We are going there to get a new pane of glass. For the window I didn't break.

I have forty-eight hours to get the Failure-mobile. And none for this.

Nor do I have time for the bowling turkey's lecture. The one he's giving me about growing up. And being responsible. And not acting like a little kid.

And not playing pretend.

So at a stop sign, I kick open the Cadillac door.

And I run.

I run anywhere. Nowhere. Away.

And into the furry side of a polar bear.

Who, on his way to the bank holding a ME WANT sign, was given everything well-meaning shop owners and food vendors could possibly think to give him. So that by the time this monstrous mammal was to crash his hulking frame through the front door of Evil's headquarters and intimidate all, he looked like this:

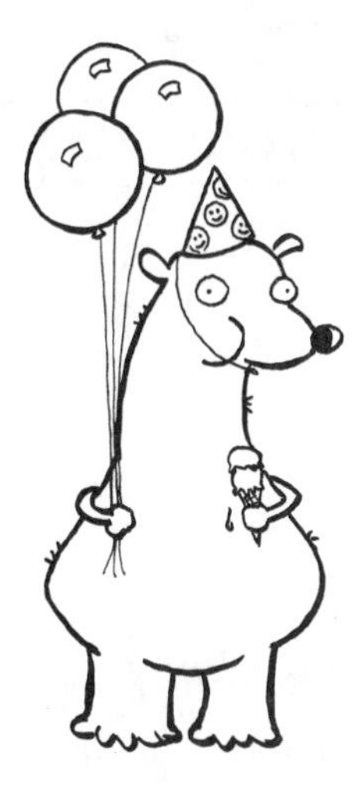

But I don't get mad. I take his paw. And we walk. Two against the world.

You can't spell *Magellan* without an *M.*

I know that because I spelled it wrong on my World Explorers history test. Here's how I spelled it:

Chang

I answered "Chang" because the question was, "Who was the first person to sail around the globe?" And I didn't know. But I did know that Chang was the most common last name in the world. So I played the odds.

It's not the first time I've done that.

Who wrote the United States Constitution?

Chang.

The bottom line is that today is Friday. And I have twenty-four hours to find the Failure-mobile.

And unless one of these explorers is going to find it, they're of no use to me.

Though I did come close to getting the question "What were the names of Christopher Columbus's three ships?"

Huey,

Dewey,

and Louie

CHAPTER 41

Seal of Approval

"'The World's Happiest Seal thought the world was a wonderful place,'" reads my mother.

"Timmy," she says, "can we stop for a minute?" She is reading one of the stories I've written for Total. But he is already asleep.

She puts down the story. “Listen. I know things haven’t been easy lately. With my job and the apartment and all the changes.”

I shrug and stare out the dark window.

“Anyway, I just want to say, Crispin told me about the talk he had with you,” she says.

Uh-oh. Here comes the mom hammer.

“And I told him he had no right.”

I look back at her.

“*I’m* your parent. Not him.” She clears the hair from my forehead. “That doesn’t mean it was right to run from the car. He spent two hours looking and couldn’t find you anywhere.”

Of course not. He is an amateur. He is not going to find a trained detective.

“Anyhow, if you want, I thought maybe we could get some seafood after the play tomorrow.

I thought your business partner might like that."

Ah, yes. The play. The one I'm going to write after she leaves my room. "My business partner would like that very much," I say. "And it's wise of you. He's one half of the agency's hiring committee."

She kisses me on the nose. And gets up to leave.

"Where you going?" I ask her.

"To bed."

"But you didn't finish the story."

She smiles and sits back down. And begins reading again.

"'The World's Happiest Seal thought the world was a wonderful place.'"

She turns the page.

CHAPTER 42

Broadway Bound

"Stop touching me!" I yell at Molly Moskins. She has both arms around me. We are standing in front of the garden shed in her large backyard.

"You sure I don't hug you here?" she asks.

"No!" I shout, smelling like tangerine.

"I *knew* we should have practiced this play," she says. "If we had practiced, it would have been wondertastical by now."

"I told you, Molly Moskins. I just finished writing it two hours ago. I was up all night." I plop back down in my director's chair. Reach for my thermos of coffee. It is all that is keeping my eyes open.

Well, that and fear. My mother will be here in an hour. I convinced her the play had to be staged here instead of the school auditorium because some of the auditorium's ceiling tiles had fallen during rehearsals.

She asked me why the school couldn't just hold it on one of their fields instead of in Molly's backyard.

I told her the female lead was a bit of a prima donna and had demanded it be in her backyard. Little did I know it would prove true.

"You didn't even write a part for Señor Burrito!" she says.

"Focus on your lines, Molly Moskins."

"It's hard to focus when Señor Burrito is sad."

I look back at Señor Burrito. I should never take my eyes off her.

“And how can you write a play called *A Segway Named Greatness* when you don’t even have a Segway?”

“The Segway is suggested, Molly. Not shown. It’s supposed to be in the big box.”

“I don’t get it,” she says.

“You’re the owner of this shop that sells

Segways. And every day I walk by your shop and tell you how much I want one. Then what do you say?"

She looks at her script. "Uhh, 'Sorry, good sir. You don't have enough money,'" she reads.

"Perfect. Then I grab the sides of my head and yell, 'SEEEEEEGGGGGWAAAAAY!'"

"What for?"

"What do you mean, 'What for?' I'm frustrated."

"Frustrated 'cause we don't hug?"

"We never hug."

"Is it 'suggested'?"

"No. Stop talking about hugs."

"Then what do we do after you yell?"

"Nothing. That's where the script ends."

"That's all you wrote?"

"*You* try writing a play in one night! You're lucky we have the sharp, witty dialogue we have."

"But I only have one line."

"Don't worry about that," I tell her. "We'll ad-lib the rest."

"What's that mean?"

"We wing it. Improvise. Say whatever comes to mind."

"I adore you!"

"What?"

"That's what came to mind."

"In the play, Molly Moskins. Ad-lib during the play. And don't say *that*. You can say anything but that."

"Okay. Uh. Hey, it's your mom!" yells an excited Molly.

"There's no mom in the play," I tell her.

"No. Coming up the driveway."

And that's when I see her. Walking up the driveway.

"Hello, Ms. Failure!" chirps Molly.

"You must be Molly," says my mother.

"Mom!" I shout. "What do you think you're doing here?"

"You said one o'clock," she replies.

"I said two o'clock."

"You said one." She takes out the tickets I had made at the copy shop.

ADMIT ONE

A Segway Named Greatness

Saturday, 1:00 p.m.

Stupid typo. Never trust your Arctic business partner to proofread.

"Yeah, well, plays *never* start on time!" I tell her. "That's why you don't see anyone else here yet. It's rude."

"Well, then fine. I'll sit and wait. Where are the chairs?"

Chairs. I knew I forgot something. "They were crushed by the falling ceiling tiles," I tell her. "You'll just have to stand. Now, give the actors some space."

My mother looks at me funny.

I rush with Molly back into the house. "Give me your phone," I tell her. "Fast."

She hands me the phone. I call Rollo. "Get here now," I tell him. "My mom showed up an hour early."

"You said two o'clock," replies Rollo.

"I know what I said. Just get here now. And tell everyone else to get here now also."

“No one else wanted to come. It’s just me.”

“I told you to ask everyone in our class except You-Know-Who.”

“I did. They said no. Do you want me to ask You-Know-Who?”

“Are you nuts?” I yell. “Alright, at least you get here. My mom’s gotta see *someone* else in the audience.”

“I can’t come until two.”

“Why not?”

“I’m studying with my tutor.”

“The Evil One’s with you now?!”

“Don’t yell at me, Timmy. If you hadn’t messed up the group tests, none of this would have happened.”

I try to respond, but I can’t. My voice is drowned out by a sputtering roar. I look out the window. And see a familiar face.

At least *someone* is dependable. I watch through Molly's kitchen window as Flo struts into the backyard. My mother spots him too. And judging a book by its cover, she moves as far away as possible from Flo the Librarian.

I return to the phone. "You listen to me, Rollo Tookus! You either get here right now or I find a way to be a part of every group test you ever take."

"You wouldn't!"

"I would."

Rollo shrieks. I turn to Molly. "C'mon. We have a play to start."

We rush out the backdoor and take our places on either side of the Segway box. I pace back and forth in front of it. As I do, I catch my mother's eye. She does not look pleased.

"'Well, I'll be,'" I declare in character. "'I sure would like to buy that Segway.'"

Molly says nothing.

"I say . . . I sure would like to buy that Segway."

Molly stands silent.

“I SAY . . . I SURE WOULD LIKE TO BUY THAT SEGWAY!” I yell.

Molly just smiles.

“Say your line, Molly,” I whisper.

“Which line?” she whispers back.

“The one we talked about,” I tell her.

She looks confused. So does my mother.

“The one we talked about!” I whisper through gritted teeth.

Her mismatched pupils widen. “I ADORE YOU, TIMMY FAILURE!” she yells, grabbing me with both of her arms. The force causes both of us to fall to the grass.

“What are you doing?” I yell, horrified.

“I’m ad-winging it!” she yells. “Just like you said.”

“Let go of me!” I yell, rolling with her across the grass. But she does not let go. And together we roll downhill to the driveway.

Where we crash into the feet of someone rotund.

It is Rollo Tookus. And behind him, the Center of Evil in the Universe.

"WHAT IS SHE DOING HERE?!" I yell.

"She wanted to see the play," says Rollo.

"Well, get her out of here! She can't see this—"

"Timmy," interrupts Rollo, "she just wants to—"

"I don't care what she wants!" I yell. "She can't—"

"It's okay, Rollo," interrupts the Evil One. "I gotta go anyway and—"

"AHHHHHHHHH!" a woman screams. It is my mother. She is running from the Moskins' automatic sprinklers. Which have just come on all across the lawn.

"Turn those off!" I shout at Molly, who is still on top of me.

"I don't know how," she says. "They're sprinklermatical."

"Then we've got to move the box!" I yell. "The water will ruin the cardboard!"

I struggle to rise. Molly hangs on to my legs. I drag both of us through the jets of water to get to the box.

But before we can get there, the box does something unexpected.

It moves toward us.

"*ROOOOARRRRRRR*," the box growls.

It is my business partner.

Who, unbeknownst to anyone, has been napping under the Segway box. And is now going to make up for the botched bank invasion by intimidating everyone here.

But he can't. Because he is now just a box with feet. And, as such, intimidates no one.

Except Señor Burrito.

Who, seeing the walking box, leaps out of my thermos and onto the face of Rollo Tookus.

Rollo panics and pulls the flying Burrito off his face. But the cat chases him. So he runs screaming into the garden shed and slams the wooden door.

Which causes the outside latch to fall and lock him in.

Rollo yells for my help. But I have no time. Because as I turn my head to avoid a jet of sprinkler water, I see my mother. Halfway down the driveway. "M-o-o-o-o-m!" I yell. But I can't move. Because Molly Moskins has both her hands around my ankle.

"LET GO, YOU IDIOT!" I yell at Molly. But as I say it, my left eye twitches. And Molly Moskins thinks I winked at her.

"YOU LOVE ME TOO!!!" she yells, pulling me back to the ground.

Smothered by kisses, I can only faintly hear the receding sound of my mother's car engine. Which is soon drowned out by the screams of Rollo.

"I DON'T WANT TO SPEND THE NIGHT IN H-E-E-E-E-E-E-E-E-R-E!!!"

Distracted by the scream, Molly turns to look at Rollo. I throw her arms off me and run. But the rest is a watery blur.

For I'm told that as I stood up, my business partner lost his balance. And fell onto my head.

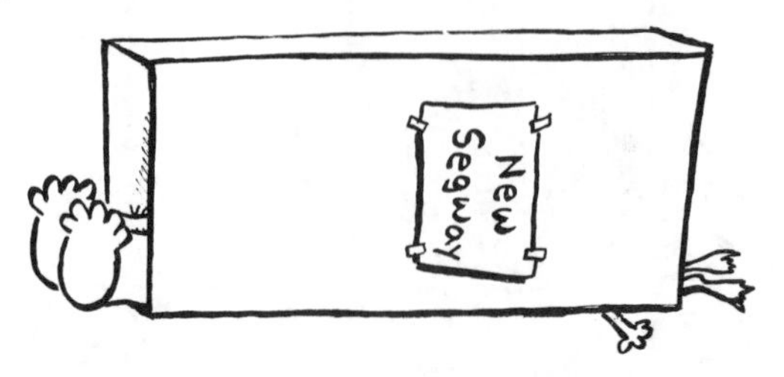

I'm further told that the same person who rescued me then unlocked the door of Rollo's garden shed prison. And scared the bejesus out of Rollo.

Who, not being a regular user of the city library, had no idea who his rescuer was.

CHAPTER 43
Kaboom

I always thought it would take one of these to bring me down:

But it didn't. It took one of these:

That's my mother. To whom, when the play ended, I was forced to confess.

Confess that I had been using the Segway.

Confess that I left it parked in front of the Hodgeses' house.

Confess that it had been stolen. And when I was done, she didn't get mad. She got silent. And with mothers, that is always the worst form of mad.

Had it been the Segway alone, perhaps I could have survived. But it wasn't. Because when she drove home that day and got the mail, she found this:

Dear Ms. Failure,

It is with regret that I inform you that your son Timmy recently scored a zero on his history exam. It is his second straight zero on an exam.

Given the low marks on both these and earlier tests, we will have no choice but to have him repeat his current grade.

Alexander Scrimshaw
Principal

And that I couldn't survive. So, in a voice of deadly calm, she gave her verdict: There would be no more investigations. There would be no more cases. There would be no more Total Failure, Inc.

But that wasn't the worst part.

That was this:

There would be no more Total.

That's right. To her, my polar bear was an extension of the agency. And anything and anyone connected to the agency was no more. I could fill pages reciting the arguments I made for keeping Total. But there's no point. None of them worked. Not a bit. So I called the only local place I knew that took polar bears.

And they agreed to take him.

And that left only the good-bye.

CHAPTER 44

(No Title)

CHAPTER 45

Key Worst

My destruction wasn't alone. Crocus imploded too.

Odd to see he had a first name. Most teachers don't. And it's too bad the educational system let him down. But these things happen.

Now he's stuck in Key West.

Without me.

Sure, I was a challenge. An obstacle. But old people need that.

Now he just has sun and the beach.

I can only imagine how sad he must be to get up in the morning and realize I'm not there.

But don't take my word for it. Look at the photo the school newspaper included.

He looks miserable.

CHAPTER 46

Going Against the Grain

Author's Note: The attached is an item of correspondence with my business partner. I include it here as a historical record of our time of incarceration, as well as to preserve it from the drool and food stains that would result were it to remain in my business partner's possession.

Day 1 of captivity

To: Total
c/o Polar Bear Exhibit
City Zoo

Dear Business Partner,

So here we are. Both imprisoned.

My cage

How long this will last, I don't know.

All I know is that I'm chained to these textbooks from the moment I get home to the moment I go to bed...

(with a break for dinner with the warden).

And I don't know what it is about these books, but they appear to be designed to send your attention elsewhere.

Like today.

I'm sitting there reading something about something when I see the pattern of the wood grain in my desk. And before I know it, I'm watching tiny me running through it like a maze.

And away goes an hour.

So I try to read again. But I hear a dog.

← Dog

Which makes me think of cars.

Which rhymes with jars.

Which hold mayonnaise.

So now I'm eating a bologna sandwich.

And _two_ hours are gone.

So I try to study again.

But my underwear is too tight.

So I have to change it.

So I look in a drawer.

And find a flashlight.

Which still works.

So I do this.

And <u>four</u> hours pass.

Until the warden checks in.

So I run to my desk.

And say things are fine.

And look at the book.

And notice the
wood
grain.

CHAPTER 47

I Get No Kick from Kickball

"I just want to know why my hamster died."

It's Max Hodges.

And he's bothering me during lunch recess.

"I can't tell you," I tell him.

"Why not?"

"Because the investigatory enterprise has been terminated by external forces."

"I don't know what that means," he says.

"That's as simply as I can put it. I'm sorry if you don't know what it means."

"Yeah, well, I know about your play," he says, smiling.

"I see," I reply in a civil tone. "So you heard it was sabotaged by a rotund ex-associate and his evil tutor?"

He shakes his head. "I heard you fell and hit your head on a sprinkler," he says.

"Mendacity!" I shout, rising to my feet.

Max Hodges scratches his head. "I don't know what that means either," he says.

"It means I have a scalawag bent on my destruction. And she is perpetrating unconscionable falsehoods."

Max Hodges looks confused.

I attempt to walk past the ignoramus, but he grabs me by the arm. "Listen, Failure. Just tell me one thing. Without saying *how* my hamster died, can you at least tell me *if* you know."

"I'm Timmy Failure," I declare. "What do you think?"

"Right now, I think you're kind of a weirdo."

Before I can reply, I am struck in the head by a kickball.

I pick up the ball. And throw it into the street.

"Sorry about the ball, Timmy. But you didn't have to throw it into traffic."

It is the new teacher. I do not know his name. So I'll call him this:

"You should try playing kickball with your classmates and me sometime," says New Guy. "It's fun."

I watch as he climbs the fence for the ball. "No, thank you," I reply.

"Why not?" he persists.

"Because you are but a shadow of the man that was Frederick Crocus. And I miss him dearly."

"Aw, c'mon," he says. "Give me a chance." He tosses me the ball.

It strikes me in the face.

"You have struck me in the face again!" I shout.

"Sorry about that," he says. "Let me show you how to catch this thing." But his lecture is mercifully interrupted by the bell for class.

"Well," I tell him, "now you can proceed to destroy the inside of my head as you've just destroyed the outside."

He laughs and walks off.

I feel a woman's hand on my shoulder. "Be nice," says Dondi Sweetwater. "Mr. Jenkins is a good guy."

"Not now," I tell the yard lady. "My lunch recess has been sabotaged."

"I saw," she says, picking up the vicious kickball. "Mind throwing this in the rec shed on your way to class?"

"Fine," I reply. "But hand it to me gently. I do not wish to be struck in the bean again."

She hands me the kickball.

"Oh, and take these too," she says, lowering her voice.

She hands me two Rice Krispies Treats.

"For the big guy," she whispers.

CHAPTER 48

Sign, Sealed, and Delivered

"He used it for packaging," I tell my business partner.

"Packaging."

It is Saturday. The one day of the week I am allowed to visit Total.

"He was sending some stupid bowling scores into some league office. Can you believe these idiots even have a *league*? Anyhow, the lunkhead doesn't want them bent! Like they're state secrets or something. So his tiny brain screams, 'Hmmm. Where can I get some card-board to stiffen the package?' And so what does he do? He pulls it off the wall. And *ships* it!"

I suppose I should back up. The lunkhead we're talking about is this guy:

And the cardboard we're talking about is this guy:

Our corporation's sign. Our respected brand. Now sitting on some forgotten trash heap in Bowlingville, USA.

"And listen to this. The guy mentions the whole thing after the fact. You know how? He says, 'Hey, did you still need that thing in the hall?' I say, 'Yes, I needed it.' And he says, 'Well, it's gone now.' And that's it! No apology. No noth—"

I stare over the railing at my business partner. "Are you listening to this?"

Total is staring at Staci, the female polar bear who shares his enclosure. But the only thing she likes is her beach ball.

"Pay attention to me!" I yell. "We've got to do something. We've got to stop this menace."

Total walks toward her. But she growls. So he rolls over like he's dead.

"Forget about the woman," I yell. "Focus on the business. We need a plan."

Total curls up in a corner of the stone enclosure.

"Listen," I tell him, "I know things look bad right now. But you've got to keep your head up. Corporations go through periods like this."

Total blinks.

"Okay, fine," I tell him. "You know what? I was gonna save this to cheer you up for later. But I'll just tell you now." I pause for dramatic effect. "Guess what's two cages to your left."

He yawns.

"Seals!" I yell. "Tasty *seals*!"

I climb the railing and point frantically to the left. "You can eat them! They're dumb and fat! Just like in the stories." But Total says nothing. So I stop yelling.

"Fine, then," I tell him. "At least this'll make you happy." I pull out the two Rice Krispies Treats from Dondi I've been saving and toss them into the enclosure. Total smells them immediately. And suddenly alert, he rises on his hind legs to catch them.

But doesn't.

Because someone quicker does.

I guess Staci does like something other than beach balls.

CHAPTER 49

You May Find Yourself Behind the Wheel of a Large Automobile

I'm driving a Cadillac.

Well, not by myself.

I'm holding the wheel while the bowling turkey works the pedals.

"I wish you wouldn't let him do that," says my mother from the backseat. "He's easily distracted."

"What's the big deal?" he says. "I'm sitting right here."

"What the heck is that thing?" I yell, turning my body to point at the world's ugliest lawn sculpture.

The car swerves sharply toward the curb. The bowling turkey grabs the wheel.

"See?" yells my mom. "He almost ran over that old man."

"What's the matter with you?" the bowling turkey shouts at me.

But nothing is wrong with me. It is the sculpture that is an offense against nature. And yet it is oddly familiar.

Those inclined toward generous interpretation might say it's a goddess rising from the sea. Or Adam touching the hand of God.

I think it's a monkey throwing a chicken.

Why someone would sculpt a monkey throwing a chicken is lost on me. Perhaps it promotes monkeys. Or belittles chickens. Either way, it almost killed a man.

So the bowling turkey drives the rest of the block. And pulls the car up to a small park on a hill.

He gets out and carries a large cooler to a picnic table.

The table is filled with his bowling buddies, their bulbous bodies straining the bending benches.

I hate these Saturday bowling gatherings. I only have so much time out of my cell, and this is a waste of it.

My mother hates them too.

So she usually makes me play Frisbee.

Which I do not enjoy.

CHAPTER 50

Our Crumbling Educational System

The class is studying photosynthesis. They are hard at work.

I am in the back row trying to build the highest eraser tower ever.

"Timmy, could you please come up here for a minute?"

It is the much-too-perky voice of New Guy. And it carries with ease to my back-row desk.

The back row is where I've been sitting ever since New Guy announced we could sit wherever we wanted. The better to hide my eraser towers.

I glare as I walk up the aisle past Rollo, who now sits in the front. We haven't spoken since he sabotaged my personal and professional life.

"You got a minute?" asks New Guy as I arrive at his large desk.

"Very few, it seems. My mother has chained me to my books."

"Well, it doesn't look like you're too hard at work at the moment," he says, pointing at my eraser tower.

"I am demonstrating the effect of your photosynthesis on eraser towers," I tell him. "So looks are deceiving."

"Listen," he says, lowering his voice, "I haven't announced this to the rest of the class, but there are parts of this photosynthesis stuff that are impossible to figure out."

I am not surprised to hear this. He is an ignoramus.

"And how is that my concern?" I reply.

"I guess it's not," he says.

"Then may I return to my photosynthesis experiments?" I ask.

"In a minute," he says. "Let me just ask you something." He looks around to make sure no one is listening.

"Your friend Rollo says people pay you to figure stuff out. Is that true?"

"Rollo?"

"Yes. Your friend Rollo."

"You mean the round fellow in the front row?" I ask.

"Yeah, I guess," he says, unsure of how to answer without insulting the round fellow in the front row.

"Well, I'm not 'friends' with the rotund boy. But yes, it is true I run a detective business that is on the verge of being a Fortune 500 company. Though at present it is shut down at the request of my interfering mother."

"I see."

"This institution is largely to blame," I remind him.

"Well, do you think if I talked to her and got her okay, you could maybe do a little research for me?"

"Fine," I tell him. "Give me a list of the topics you need researched by the close of school today. But be aware that if my mother refuses to grant permission, it will have to be an all-cash transaction. I can't risk a paper trail."

"Don't worry," he says. "I'll get her approval first."

As I return to my seat, I stare at the sea of upturned faces whose education will suffer mightily at the hands of this charlatan.

But that's their problem. Because business is business.

And it's every man for himself in this monkey-throw-chicken world.

CHAPTER 51

No Teacher Left Behind

To: Total
c/o Polar Bear Exhibit

It is a good thing my innate greatness came with humility. Otherwise, I might be tempted to brag. Instead, I'll just say this:

This week I saved the entire nation's educational system.

But I don't have time to talk about it.

Suffice it to say we have a new teacher. He is an ignoramus.

As such, I must figure everything out for him.

So far, I have unraveled the mysteries of the French Revolution, fractions, and photosynthesis.

Then I explained them all to him in terms his tiny brain could comprehend:

And get this:

These are all paying cases.

Well, they're *supposed* to be. He hasn't actually paid yet.

But here's the important part:

My hypocritical mother has **approved** of these transactions.

That's right. It looks like the warden has finally recognized the foolishness of shutting down a financial empire.

But I don't have time to discuss this.

Instead, I have to unravel the mystery of conjunctions.

On a personal note, please refrain from your obsession with Staci the polar bear. In your battle for her affections, you have lost to a beach ball.

← Beach ball

Instead, focus on the reemergence of the business.

A business that may soon be needing you.

To perform an unpleasant task.

CHAPTER 52

Read All About It

I am awakened by a screaming woman.

It is the second time I have been awakened by a screaming woman this week.

My mother hands me my report on the French Revolution. There is a large *B* written at the top of it. "I can't believe it!" my mother shouts. "It's a *B*! Your new teacher gave you a *B*!"

"Our educational system's shortcomings are no cause for celebration," I tell her. "The imbecile's lucky he has me. May I return to bed?"

"And that's not even the best part, Timmy! Mr. Jenkins included a note that said you're improving in almost all your subjects! I bet if you keep it up, they'll reconsider making you repeat the grade!"

I yawn.

"Now, nothing's guaranteed, of course. I'm sure you'd still have to keep up these grades. But it's paying off, Timmy. All that studying. It's paying off!"

"I do research, Mother," I remind her. "And it's for the business. A business you all but crushed."

"Well, I don't care what you say. We need to celebrate. Let's go out to a big lunch together. Wherever you want. Would you like that?"

"I'd like to sleep in. It's Saturday."

"It's almost noon. C'mon. You'll love it."

I sit up in bed. "What I'd love is—" I stop myself.

"What?" she asks. "Say it."

"What I'd love is to get my business back."

She sits next to me on the foldout bed. "I know," she says.

"The one client you've permitted me is a deadbeat debtor," I tell her. "Who can run a business like that?"

She puts her arm around me. "Well, no promises, okay? But why don't we discuss all that at lunch?"

"Fine. At a lunch teleconference?" I ask.

"Yes. A lunch teleconference. Now, get out of bed."

I fold the bed into the couch and walk into the kitchen. I am greeted by a bowling turkey.

"Hear we're going for a big lunch, kid," he says from behind a newspaper.

"Afterward, we can head out to the park to see my bowling pals," he says. "How's that for a day?"

I reminisce about those glorious Saturdays.

"Just give me about fifteen minutes to wax

the car," he says, getting up from the table. "Then we can leave. Want the paper?" He holds out the newspaper.

"No," I tell him.

"No, *thank you,*" he corrects me. And lays it in front of me anyway.

I watch as he leaves the apartment, his polyester pant legs swooshing against each other. The door slams shut behind him. And that's when I see it. The most disturbing newspaper headline of all time.

WEALTHY DONOR MAKES LARGE CONTRIBUTION TO CITY ZOO

ZOO WILL RENAME POLAR BEAR EXHIBIT AFTER DONOR'S FAMILY MEMBER

Not disturbing enough for you?

Behold the family member.

CHAPTER 53

Where Evil Resides

I immediately understand everything.

First she gets her father to make a cash contribution to the zoo.

Then they get the polar bear exhibit renamed.

Then she gets my polar bear.

It is all as clear as the sheen on the bowling turkey's Cadillac. The same person who stole my Failuremobile is now going to steal my business partner.

I rush out of the apartment to find the bowling turkey. "I want to go to your stupid picnic now!" I yell.

"What?" says the bowling turkey, buffing his car's precious fender.

"Your picnic thing. At the park. I love it. Let's leave now."

My mother is standing next to him. "You don't want to go to lunch?" she asks.

"No!" I shout. "The picnic! I love the picnic!"

She pauses. "Fine," she says. "I'll get my purse." She stares at me with one eyebrow raised as she walks back into the apartment building. She returns with her purse. The bowling turkey opens the front passenger door for her.

"No, no. Not her. Me," I say, stepping in front of her. "I want to sit in the front seat."

"Why you rude little—" the bowling turkey starts to shout at me. My mother stops him.

"It *is* his day," she says.

"Fine," he says, "but you're not steering again, kid, if that's what you're thinking."

"I know," I tell him. "I just like to sit in front. I love it when it's all clean."

He stares at me for a moment, then throws the buffing rag into the trunk. "Okay," he says. "Get in."

We begin driving. At a stoplight, he puts the car in neutral and revs the engine. "She sure does love being waxed," he tells me, referring to his inanimate car. "Listen to that engine."

I stare at his foot pushing the accelerator.

He pops the car into drive. The Cadillac's wheels screech down the street. A street we didn't take the last time. "This isn't how you go to the park!" I yell. "Go the way we went before."

"What do you care?" asks the bowling turkey.

"It's *my* celebration!" I remind him.

He looks back at my mother.

"I guess it is his celebration," my mother says apologetically.

"Fine," says the bowling turkey. "How'd we go there last time?"

I indicate the way. He follows my direction.

And a block from the park, I see it. "Stop the car!" I yell.

"What now?" he yells.

"That house with the sculpture!" I shout. "There it is!"

"Not this again," my mom says from the backseat.

"What the heck is it with you and that stupid thing?" says the bowling turkey. "Get over it, already."

"It's just ugly," I say, staring out at it. "It ruins the look of the whole house."

"Weirdo," he says.

I see my mom frown in the rearview mirror. I'm not sure at whom.

We drive up the hill to the park. "Don't park here," I tell him. "Park there." I point to the spot on the other side of the street where we parked last time.

"You're really pushing it, kid. You know that?" he says.

"I just like to do everything the way we always do it," I tell him.

He takes a deep breath and swings the car into the spot across the street.

"Everyone's gotta carry something," says the bowling turkey, opening his trunk. He grabs a cooler and a six-pack of Coke and hands my mom a folding chair. He closes the trunk and locks the car.

"You take this," my mom says to me, handing me the soda.

"I can take more stuff than that," I tell both of them. "Give me the keys and I'll make a few more trips."

The bowling turkey stares at me.

“It’s the least I can do for being such a pain on the way over,” I say.

“Fine,” he says, tossing me the keys. “But don’t rest anything on the trunk. You’ll scratch it.”

I wait until they’ve walked through the park gate and out of view.

And hurl the soda cans to the ground.

With the sound of hissing carbonation receding behind me, I sprint toward the house at the bottom of the hill.

I stop at the edge of its front lawn.

And grab the Evil One’s detective log from my back pocket.

And turn to the last page.

And there it is.

The sketch of the art piece she did for our school's open house.

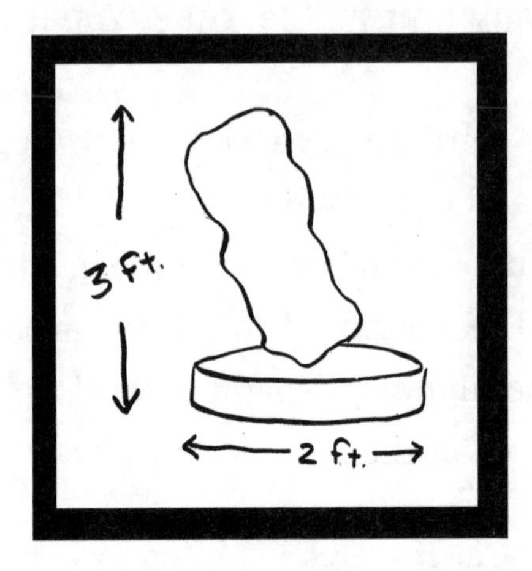

The same one that's now on her front lawn.

I have found it. The fortress. The citadel. The home of the person who will not be stealing my polar bear.

I run back up the hill toward the Cadillac. Shaking, I open the car door and jump into the driver's seat. I try to recall everything I saw the bowling turkey do on the drive over.

First step, ignition. My hands fumble through the ring of keys. I find the right one. I put it in the ignition. And turn the key.

The engine roars to life.

Second step, the gas pedal. I reach my leg down as far as it will go and push it with my foot.

The engine revs as it did at the stoplight. Only deeper and louder.

Parked on this side of the street, I can peer over the steering wheel and just see the doomed house that lies straight ahead at the bottom of the hill. I need only pop the car into gear and give it the slightest of gas.

I rev the engine again.

I am entranced by its roar.

CHAPTER 54

We've Got to Fight the Powers That Be (at the Bottom of the Hill)

But I don't act. I can't. I'm just one half of a team. A man without backup. A man without muscle. I must get Total.

I think about taking the car. But no. Can't risk it. Straight down a hill? Sure. But through town to the zoo? No way.

I hop out of the car and run for the zoo.

But I stop at the edge of the block. It won't work. That bear is trapped behind a twenty-foot moat. *He can't jump twenty feet.* He can't jump a can of beans.

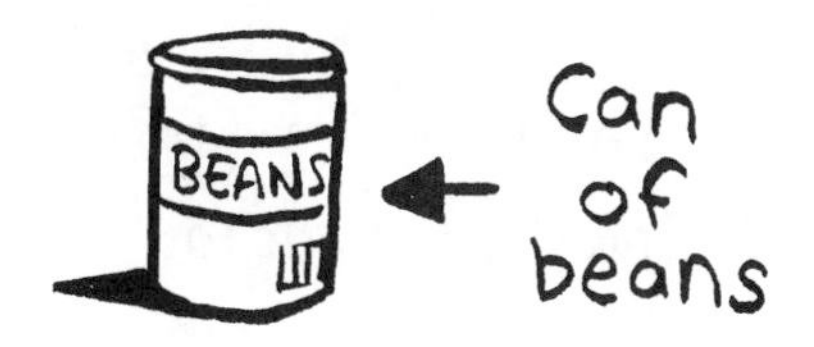

Then it hits me.

Not the can of beans. Something better.

I turn on my heels and run for the school.

Where I see the Saturday soccer games.

I run through three different games until I find the one I need.

I sprint for the woman standing at its center.

"What are you doing?" Dondi Sweetwater asks me. "I'm officiating a game."

"I need the goods!" I tell her.

"The what?" Dondi yells.

A kid dribbling the soccer ball brushes past me. "The *goods*!" I remind her.

"Oh," she says, ducking under a kicked ball. "Why do you need some now?"

"Never mind that," I cut in. "I need them."

"Okay," she says as a boy smashes into her thigh. "Look in the red cooler over there. I have a box of them. I was saving them for the kids here, but—"

I don't hear the end of the sentence. For I am struck in the face by an assassin's soccer ball.

Dazed but conscious, I boldly stay on my feet and run for the sideline.

Where I find the red cooler. And grab the goods.

And sprint for the zoo.

But I have no money for admission. So I duck under the ticket window. And rush for the Arctic mammal section. There, asleep in the corner, is Total.

I tear open the box of Rice Krispies Treats and hold two high over my head.

I watch across the wide moat as Total's nose twitches. And his right eye opens. And his left.

Then he rises on his hind legs and roars.

And is pushed down with one paw by Staci.

Who still manages to hold the beach ball with her free hand.

Staci growls for the Rice Krispies Treats. Total cowers and retreats toward the far wall of the enclosure.

So I do the only thing I still can. Which is to grab the entire box and hold it high over my head.

It is a volume of Rice Krispies Treats that Total has never seen before.

And he explodes like a cannonball.

Straight across the hard stone floor of the enclosure.

Over the swimming pool.

Past the left side of Staci, who drops her beach ball as she sees:

Total leaping over a twenty-foot moat.

Before I can stop him, he is using both paws to scarf down the treats, wrappers still on.

"Eat on the way!" I yell. "We have work to do!" I hop on his back and ride toward the park, tossing treats in his mouth along the way. It is the fastest I have ever seen him run.

We run past the Evil One's house. Up the slope toward the park. Straight for the gleaming Cadillac.

Total dives into the backseat. I turn the ignition and rev the engine. And pop the car into gear.

It explodes down the hill.

This is for the CCIA.

Past the parked cars.

This is for the theft of my cases.

Past the green lawns.

This is for the Failuremobile.

Up and over the curb.

This is for Total.

And through the living-room window.

In a thunderous explosion of brick and wood, metal and glass.

The car comes to rest at the foot of a living-room table. Steam hisses from the Cadillac's broken radiator.

As the smoke from the debris clears, I peer through the shattered windshield. But I do not see the Evil One.

I turn back to Total. "We are in the correct house, right?" I ask.

He says nothing.

I look back through the large hole in the wall, where the now-shattered sculpture lies on the lawn. "That's the sculpture," I say. "This *has* to be the house."

I scan for any sign of the Weevil Bun. I see none.

And then I hear a voice from the backseat. "Why are you doing this?" Total asks.

"What?" I say.

"Why are you doing this?" I hear again.

"Why am I doing what?" I answer.

"Why are you doing this?"

CHAPTER 55

Guess Who's Coming to Dinner

It is my mom. And she is angry.

"Why are you doing this?!" she yells.

I am behind the wheel of the Cadillac. It is parked at the top of the hill. The engine is on. And I have not driven it anywhere.

"So this is why you wanted the keys?" she asks. "To rev the engine?"

I can see Crispin running toward me from the park gate. "What in the—? What do you think you're doing?" He reaches in and turns the engine off.

"I just wanted to hear that sound again," I tell him. "The one you made at the light."

"See?" my mom yells at him. "This is what you get. Letting him grab the wheel. Showing off with your stupid car."

“This is what *I* get?” he yells back. “You’re the one that coddles him.”

“Coddles him?”

“Coddles him! Why do you think he still plays all the pretend games? I’m just trying to teach him to be a man!” He turns the key in the ignition. The car roars back to life.

“Rev the engine, kid! Go for it!”

“You’re ridiculous,” my mother yells at him. “This has nothing to do with being a man!”

Crispin opens the passenger door and sits beside me. “You want to hear the sound I made at the light?” he says to me.

“Turn the car off, Crispin!” shouts my mother.

“Go ahead! Put it in neutral and rev the engine! It’s okay. It won’t go anywhere.”

I put it in neutral and rev the engine.

“Stop it, Crispin!” my mom yells.

“Now pop it into drive, kid. C’mon! I’ve got one foot over the brake! The tires will squeal. C’mon, now!”

“I don’t want to,” I tell him. My left eye twitches.

"You gonna be a little kid your whole life?" he shouts at me. "Pop it into gear! I got the brakes! Pop it into gear!"

My mother runs for the driver's door. Just as Crispin pops the car into gear.

But he doesn't slam on the brakes.

Because he falls out his open door.

"TIMMMMMY!" my mother yells as the car thunders down the hill. Crispin jumps to his feet and starts sprinting for the car.

But it's too late. The Cadillac is tearing down the hill. Headed like a missile toward the home of Corrina Corrina. I strain with my right foot to hit the brakes but I slide off the seat and under the dashboard. I curl into a ball. And brace for the impact. . . .

But what happened next I don't know.

Because all I remember is waking up in a cloud of smoke and hearing the sound of adults trying to climb through the large hole in the wall.

And looking out through the cracked windshield at a plastic-covered recliner and a person sitting in it. A person eating a TV dinner.

And it is then that I have a moment of clarity.

Of Corrina Corrina.

And how she kisses up to people in authority. And gives them gifts.

Like ugly handmade sculptures they can put on their lawns.

Such as the one she gave to this guy.

The man sitting across from me.

Freshly back from Key West.

CHAPTER 56

Trouble in the Red Zone

There's not much to tell you about the police station. Except it was the last time my mother and I saw this guy:

Only he didn't look like that. He looked like this:

He's in trouble for reckless endangerment of a something-or-other. Cops grilled him bad. Really rattled the poor stiff. Not me. I've seen the inside of so many police stations I can practically walk 'em with my eyes closed. All comes with the job. And I knew the boys in blue would insist on calling me Detective Failure. So I tried to put them at ease.

The chief asked me to give a quick statement about the crash. So I did. No frills. No hysterics. Just the facts. I knew how these G-men liked it.

When I was done, I took a quick swig of the chocolate milk they gave me (all out of scotch, they said) and told them to go easy on the bowling turkey. Poor guy's just misguided, I told 'em.

Afterward, they offered me a tour of the station. Didn't really want it. But I humored them.

We walked past the booking desk. Past the holding cells. Through the cops' break room.

It was nice. But nothing to write Mom about.

Until we got to the impound lot outside.

And found something to write Mom about.

I recognized it by the scratch I'd given it when I crashed into Rollo one time.

“How’d you get this?” I asked the lieutenant who was giving me the tour.

He glanced at the tag hanging from the handlebars. “Parked in a tow-away zone,” he said.

I thought back to the Hodgeses’ curb. Sure, it was red. But no self-respecting cop would do a tow-away job on a detective’s vehicle.

“That can’t be,” I told the lieutenant. “This vehicle was stolen. Stolen and brought here. Probably by someone this high.” I held my hand four feet from the ground.

“An elf?” he asked, making himself laugh.

“This is no joke, Lieutenant. She’s a girl. Black hair. Ethics of a mule.”

“I don’t know anything about that,” said the lieutenant.

"I saw the vehicle!" I insisted. "Behind a bank! It was contraband!"

The lieutenant shook his head. "Kid, I don't know what you're talking about. These things all look alike." He walked back toward the police station.

"You don't understand!" I shouted.

"Thanks for your time," he said, closing the back station door behind him.

"It's a cover-up!" I yelled.

But he was already gone.

CHAPTER 57

For Whom the Timmyline Tolls

"The only reason I told your mom there wasn't a play was because *I didn't know* you were doing one. You never told me."

It is Charles "Rollo" Tookus. Standing outside my apartment window. And we are sorting through unfinished business.

"And I didn't *bring* my tutor to the play.

She insisted," he said. "And besides, how about what *you* did on all those group tests and with the bank safe and—"

"Whoa, whoa, whoa," I tell him. "The bank safe was your fault."

"Fine," he answers. "But not the group test."

I can tell he's looking for an apology. So I give him one.

"Mistakes were made," I say.

Rollo smiles. "Friends?" he asks.

"Let's not get soft," I tell him. "Come on up. I want to show you my new—"

But my answer is cut short by the crack of a sharpshooter's bullets against my window. I dive below the windowsill with lightning-quick reflexes.

When the shooting ends, I look out the window.

And see Molly Moskins.

Holding Hershey's Kisses.

"Kisses for my love!" she shouts up at the window.

"Leave me alone, Molly Moskins!" I yell. "You've terrorized this town enough!"

"But I have cases!" she yells, throwing me another Hershey's Kiss.

It strikes me in the eye. "Ahhhhh! Look what you've done! You've blinded me!"

"Blinded you?" she asks. "Are you sure? So you can't see this?"

She lifts the cuffs of her pants. She has bare ankles.

"Someone stole my socks!" she yells.

"Someone *globalnational*!" she adds.

But I don't have time to answer. Because there's a knock at the apartment door.

I open the door and see Rollo.

"How's your eye?" he asks.

"Not good," I tell him. "It feels as though she's damaged the fibula."

"That's part of your leg," he says.

"You know nothing," I tell him.

"So what did you want to show me?" he asks.

"Follow me," I say.

As we walk, I hear more Hershey's Kisses ping against the windowpane.

"So my mom cleared out all her clothes,"

I tell him, showing him my mother's bedroom closet. "She says I can use it for now. She'll keep her stuff somewhere else."

"It's smaller than the last one you had," he says.

"Of course it's smaller, you idiot. I *wanted* it smaller. My mom says I can't do as much detective work as before. Downsizing sends the message that I'm listening to her."

"Oh," he answers.

"Besides," I tell him, "I'm still missing my business partner, so the payroll's cut by fifty percent."

"Hey, speaking of that," Rollo asks, "did you ever give my tutor back her detective log?"

"No," I said. "But my mother did. She found it in the backseat of the Cadillac and returned it to the Weevil Bun's father."

"Did you read it?"

"'Course I read it. Waste of time. All personal stuff. I'm sure it bored her father to tears."

He started to ask another question. But I couldn't talk to him anymore.

Because the Timmyline was ringing.

CHAPTER 58

Elementary, My Dear Gunnar

"You're late," says Gunnar. "I called you half an hour ago."

"Could not be helped," I tell him. "Forces beyond the corporation's control have forbid further use of the Failuremobile."

"Yeah," he answers, laughing, "I heard it got towed and your mom had to pay some big fine to get it back and—"

"It was stolen, you imbecile! Stolen! I saw it with my own eyes behind the Evil One's headquarters."

"There's more than one Segway in the world, Timmy."

"Is that why you called me here? To waste my time?"

"Relax, Timmy," he says. "I just wanted to know what happened to my case. You never figured it out."

"Oh, I didn't?" I answer knowingly.

"Well, did you?" he asks.

So I proceed to lay out all of the evidence. Step by step. With clockwork precision. His brother Gabe's room. The empty pumpkin. The chocolate smeared around Gabe's face. The alibi.

"So it was Gabe?" he asks as I finish.

I try not to laugh. "Gunnar," I say, "do you remember all the candy you told me was missing?"

"I think so."

"List it," I tell him.

He thinks back. "Okay, uh, there were two Mars bars, a Twix, uh, seven 3 Musketeers, five Kit Kats, eleven Almond Joys, and, hmmm, five Snickers, an Abba-Zaba and uh . . . "

I stop him. "Say this last part slow."

He stares at me with the dull eyes of an amateur. "Eight Hershey's Kisses?" he says.

"Bingo," I tell him.

"Bingo?" he asks.

"Bingo," I say.

CHAPTER 59

Total Victory

"Are you ready?" my mother yells from her bedroom.

I'm reading the mail on the kitchen table. "What's this one?" I ask, holding up a postcard.

"We're gonna be late," my mom says, walking into the kitchen. "We've already postponed this lunch reservation once. Do you want to celebrate your grades or not?"

"It's from Crocus," I tell her.

"I know," she says. "He got a lot of insurance money for his house. So he sold it and moved."

I read the back of the postcard.

"Well, now, that's immature," I say, putting down the card.

"Are you ready or not?" she asks, "We're gonna be—"

She is cut off by the squeal of a truck's brakes. I stare out the kitchen window at a large, nondescript truck.

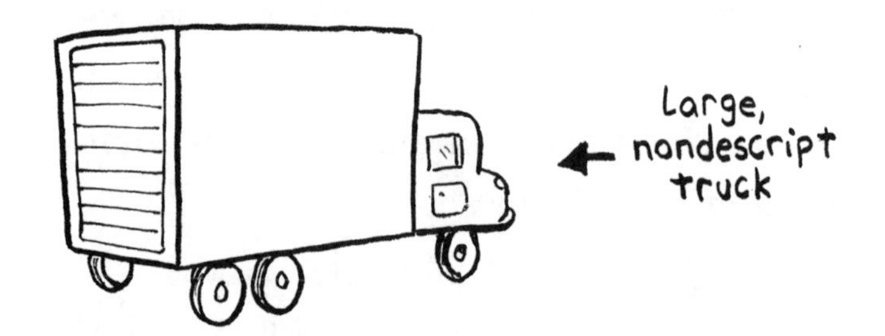

The driver gets out and walks toward our apartment building. I meet him halfway up the walk.

"You Timmy Failure?" he asks, checking a clipboard.

"I am he," I tell him. "The owner of Total Failure, Inc. I presume you have a case."

"A case?" he says. "I don't got a case."

He swings open the truck's large roll-up door. "I got a bear."

Total leaps from the back of the truck and knocks me to the grass. It is an unprofessional display of affection, licking, and drool.

I hug him back.

"Zoo says he don't play too good with others. Guess he did something to make some other bear real mad."

Total runs back into the truck.

And returns with something to show me.

CHAPTER 60

It Begins Again

My mother said our lunch was to celebrate grades. But that was a ruse. The truth was we were there to celebrate the rebirth of Total Failure, Inc. For I had brilliantly solved all my cases.

The Tiny Person who'd TP'ed the Weber home? Molly Moskins.

The larcenist who'd lifted the load of candy? Molly Moskins.

And the cause of death for the Hodgeses' hamster? Elementary, my dear friend. Hamsters are rodents. Cats kill rodents. And who owns a cat?

That's right. Molly Moskins's Señor Burrito is a murderer.

Other than that, I really don't want to talk about the celebration lunch because the whole thing pretty much got ruined.

For one thing, my mom made me invite Rollo. That was stupid because his GPA had recently slipped to 4.55 and his head was shaking like the top of a pressure cooker.

Then there was Total.

My mom let me order him halibut. (It was the closest thing we could find to seal.) But what a waste. The poor slob spent the entire lunch behind the restaurant.

To top it all off, we saw Flo. Eating alone at the lunch counter.

That was okay with me. But not for my mom. To her, he's still that "strange guy at the play." And I have to admit that he *did* look intimidating. Especially given the fact that he was reading another book on how to kill things.

But what destroyed the entire event—made my blood pressure rise and my fists clench—were the two people in the back corner booth. One was You-Know-Who. I'll just put the little black box over her head again.

And the other was her father.

My mom said they were coloring a kids' menu together. I didn't see that. But I did see she was smiling and laughing.

Which could only mean one thing. . . .

She was plotting more evil.

The only thing better than reading my memoirs is reading **MORE** of my memoirs.

Turn the page to start reading the second volume. . . .

Available in hardcover and paperback and as an e-book

www.candlewick.com

A Prologue That Will Most Likely Make Sense Later

Of all the items that can clog your plumbing, an overweight Arctic mammal is probably the worst.

Because while a good plumber can clear your pipes of a spoon or a hair ball or a bar of soap, it is much harder to remove one of these:

That, you see, is a polar bear.

And today he is stuck in a different kind of pipe.

The Tube O' Terror.

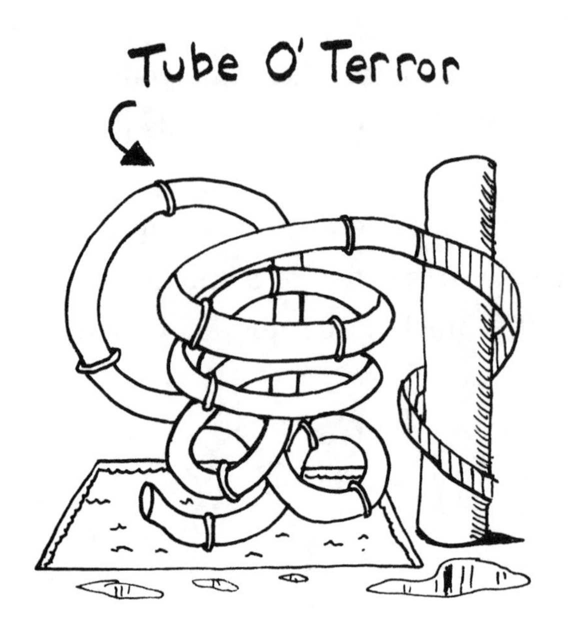

The Tube O' Terror is the world's fastest, curviest waterslide.

But it is not fast today.

Because it is clogged.

Clogged by an overeager polar bear who was much too plump to ride.

And yet somebody let him.

An excerpt from *Timmy Failure: Now Look What You've Done*

And that is where the bribery comes in.

Because a polar bear who fails to get his way will charm. And a polar bear who fails to charm will deceive. And a polar bear who fails to deceive will grab a big wad of dollar bills from his pocket and wink.

Because that is how the world works.

And then this will happen.

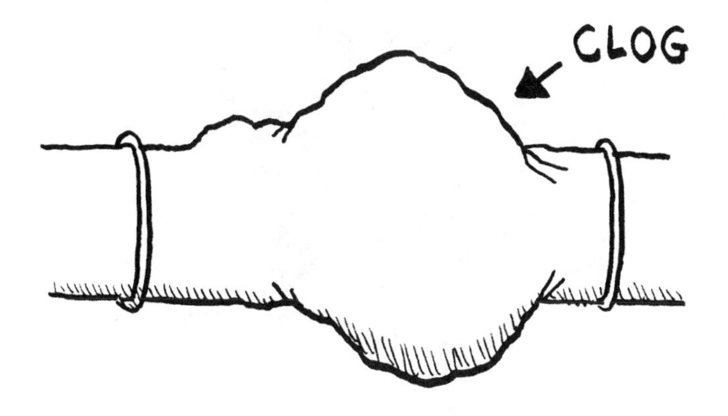

And if you are a world-class detective who just so happens to be tied to that polar bear and had no choice but to follow him down the slide, you are in trouble.

Deep, unbreathable trouble.

Because the rushing water keeps coming.

An excerpt from *Timmy Failure: Now Look What You've Done*

And with the polar bear's big bottom acting as a plug, the water has nowhere to go but back up the tube.

Which is where I am.

Trapped underwater.

And not very happy about it.

CHAPTER 1
A Head Is a Terrible Thing to Not Have

Carl Kobalinski is not the smartest person in the world.

But try telling that to the woman in the checkered vest.

"Maury's Museum of World Records is now closed," she says. "And you need to go home."

"But look at this thing," I tell her. "It's an outrage."

"What is?" she asks.

"This," I say, pointing directly at the statue.

"Kid, I get eight dollars an hour to walk around this museum and make sure no one breaks anything. If you have a problem with what's in it, tell someone else."

"I've got a problem, all right. Lies, lies, and more lies. Everyone knows who the smartest person is."

An excerpt from *Timmy Failure: Now Look What You've Done*

"Wonderful," she mumbles, rubbing her temples.

"It's me," I say.

"Good for you," she says, pushing me toward the exit with one hand. "Now let me show the smartest person in the world how a door works."

I am suddenly tempted to pull rank.

Reveal that I am this guy:

It is a name so recognizable that she would instantly know it as that of the founder, president, and CEO of the greatest detective agency in the town, probably the state. Perhaps the nation.

But I don't pull rank.

I do something smarter.

I climb Carl Kobalinski and try to yank down his sign.

“What do you think you’re doing?” screams the museum woman.

“I’m saving the credibility of your institution!” I retort.

But I’m not.

An excerpt from *Timmy Failure: Now Look What You’ve Done*

Because I can't reach the sign without jumping. And I am nine feet above the ground.

So I do what only the smartest person in the world would think to do.

I jump.

Only to learn that while Carl may have had a strong brain, his statue does not have a strong neck.

And as I jump, it snaps. Sending both me and Carl's overrated head tumbling.

Straight to the museum floor.

Where I hear another snap.

This one in my leg.

And say the only logical thing I can to the museum woman leaning over me:

"Now look what you've done."

An excerpt from *Timmy Failure: Now Look What You've Done*

CHAPTER 2

The Cast That Limits Me

When you're lying in bed with a broken right leg, you can either cry or write your memoirs.

And Timmy Failure doesn't cry.

So here are my memoirs:

I was born.

I exhibited greatness.

I founded an empire.

An excerpt from *Timmy Failure: Now Look What You've Done*

And that empire was achieved despite the many obstacles around me.

Such as Obstacle No. 1.

That's my mother.

She's a kind enough person. But she has her weaknesses.

Like insisting I attend this place:

An excerpt from *Timmy Failure: Now Look What You've Done*

Now, school is fine for those who need it.

But for those touched by greatness, it is a debilitating nuisance.

Then there's Obstacle No. 2.

His name is Total. He is a fifteen-hundred-pound polar bear.

He was raised in the Arctic. But his home melted like an ice cube in the sun. And he wandered 3,000 or so miles to my house.

So I gave him a job.

And for the first six months, he was the most reliable polar bear I've ever employed.

Then he revealed his true colors.

It was a betrayal so profound that I do not wish to discuss it.

So let me just say this.

If a polar bear ever works very hard for you in the first six months of employment, keep this one thing in mind:

IT IS A RUSE.

Do NOT make him a partner at your detective agency.

Do NOT agree to change the name of the agency from "Failure, Inc." to "Total Failure, Inc."

And, hey, while I'm issuing warnings, do NOT model your life after the person who is Obstacle No. 3.

An excerpt from *Timmy Failure: Now Look What You've Done*

His name is Rollo Tookus. He is my best friend. And he is boring.

Boring because all he cares about is grades.

So that's all the description he gets.

And I will fill the space he otherwise would have gotten in these memoirs with a drawing of my face.

An excerpt from *Timmy Failure: Now Look What You've Done*

More memoirs. More greatness.

YOU CAN'T FAIL TO HAVE FUN AT
www.timmyfailure.com

www.candlewick.com

STEPHAN PASTIS is the creator of *Pearls Before Swine,* an acclaimed comic strip that appears in more than seven hundred U.S. newspapers, boasts a devoted following, and hit #1 on the *New York Times* bestseller list with the 2011 compilation *Larry in Wonderland*. Stephan Pastis took an unusual route to becoming a best-selling comics creator: he went to law school. Hopelessly bored sitting in class at UCLA, he found himself sketching the character Rat. Creative inspiration followed him through graduation in 1993 to his first law firm job in San Francisco, and *Pearls Before Swine* was born in 1997. *Timmy Failure: Mistakes Were Made* is his first book for young readers, and is followed by *Timmy Failure: Now Look What You've Done* and *Timmy Failure: We Meet Again*. He lives in northern California.